BLACK COFFEE NIGHT

BLACK COFFEE NIGHT

SHORT STORIES

BY

EMILY SCHULTZ

Emily Schultz

impolsion
imprint

INSOMNIAC PRESS

Edited by Stephen Cain
Copy edited by Adrienne Weiss
Designed by Jonathan Blackburn
Cover and author photographs by Brian Joseph Davis

National Library of Canada Cataloguing in Publication Data

Schultz, Emily, 1974 –
    Black Coffee Night

Includes bibliographical references.
ISBN 1-894663-26-8

    I. Title.

PS8587.C5474B52 2002   C813'.54   C2002-903819-7

The publisher gratefully acknowledges the support of the Canada Council, the Ontario Arts Council and the Department of Canadian Heritage through the Book Publishing Industry Development Program.

The author gratefully acknowledges the financial support of the Ontario Arts Council during the completion of this book.

Printed and bound in Canada

Insomniac Press
192 Spadina Avenue, Suite 403
Toronto, Ontario, Canada, M5T 2C2
www.insomniacpress.com

FOAM
9

THE PHYSICAL ACT OF LEAVING
15

THE VALUE OF X
25

WHAT IS SARAH CHATEL THINKING?
41

THE AMATEURS
51

ACCESSORIES
69

WATERING THE DARK
77

SUBSTITUTE
85

THE MOTHERS
99

MEASUREMENT LISTINGS IN THE CATALOGUE OF
MEMORY
117

THE YEARS OF THE STRAWBERRY CIRCUS
141

Eat, drink, talk, she seemed to whisper as she placed the menu into the visitor's hand, as if she were giving them the secret to all delights, and often they moved aside to make room and said: "Renate, sit down, have a drink with us."

Animator, bringing animation to silent tables, staying long enough to light the candles.

They arrived in disparate costumes, formal and informal...

...Nothing seemed to belong to them organically, to be stamped with their own identity, but no one seemed to expect that. Even the painters and writers wore disguises which outdid Venetian masked balls. The beards of men shipwrecked for years on desert isands, the unmatched clothes from thrift shops, the girls with hair uncombed, and black cotton stockings, and eyes painted a tubercular violet. In this costume they meant to convey a break with conventions, with the stylish mannequins in Beverly Hills shop windows, but it created the impression of merely another uniform, which they bore self-consciously, and it did not portray freedom, nonchalance. They wore them stiffly, as if on display, like extras for a Bohemian scene, proclaiming: look at me.

All of them were impatient to drink the dissolvent remedy which would loosen the disguise, disintegrate the self-conscious shell, to drink until the lower depths of their nature would rise to the surface...

from *Collages* by Anaïs Nin

This book is for my old gang.
There is no true representation.
Only love beyond recognition.

FOAM

foam (fōm), n. 1. *a collection of minute bubbles formed on the surface of a liquid by agitation, fermentation, etc. 2. the froth of perspiration formed on the skin of a horse or other animal from great exertion. 3. froth formed in the mouth.*

THE NIGHT IS a saucer catching all the spills. Words like sugar granules collect in crusted brown rivers as hours clink and clatter away beneath the movement of hands.

Single shot in white cup. Double shot in black, let run through. He makes coffee all evening, reminding himself of the price increase, to ring it in ten cents higher than usual. People come in. They order things. He nods. He gives them all the same thing, the only difference being more or less. He pulls the flatware out of the sink. The dishwasher is broken again. Sorting the long spoons from the short he notices his fingers have puckered.

She stays late at the library, pretending to do research when all she really wants to do is look at the pictures. In other study carrels, under the thumbs of people she can't see, the pages turn, hissing and whispering, *What is this? Who are you? Where have we been stored all these months?*

She skips supper and gets a coffee to go from the kiosk in the lobby. It's been sitting on the burner. Her teeth worry the rim of the Styrofoam as she walks and she feels the urge to bite clear through it. She goes out to the bus stop, the shelter a waiting tank. As the bus lurches with her inside, street lights fall at random past the window, giant chunky white, streaking towards the dirty glass.

When he finishes his shift at the café downtown, he goes home, and lies against her, fitting top to bottom, just so, like a thing set down properly. Some nights there is steam on his lips and he wraps both hands around her body, holds onto her neck and the handle of her hip, pouring everything inside him into her. Other nights he sits too long and goes cold, beginning to think of himself as a device and not really a man at all. She, as something that constantly needs refilling. He tries to crawl over her, but she wakes and says she wants to consume him, and so they do, stir each other up, gulp at one another with long grey grimaces. He's glad he can't see her face.

In the dark, she thinks only of the representation of men in classical sculpture. The hard surface of male statues in museums she has visited. Thinkers and kings, both mythical and anonymous figures, larger than life and with humourously miniature genitalia. He, on the other hand, is a small man with a large member. She thinks of her grandmother's bone china, its handles unnecessary flourishes for fingers to wrap around, the handles almost bigger than the insides of the bowls. Where he sleeps beside her, she examines his protruding cheekbones, skin translucent in the pale square of light seeping through the window. The street light is a sugar cube that dissolves in sleep. He is the figurine of a man, made for her bedside table.

In the morning, the street is being jackhammered up. Their heads feel cracked against the pillows. The night has been dropped into a murky puddle on the floor beside them. He is aware of himself as all smell, all smoke. She feels all the words have been sucked out of her.

There is a sadness here but they won't acknowledge it. They will rinse themselves off, squatting among the black tile with white porcelain bathroom fixtures, the old-fashioned tub with the claw feet, the shower nothing but a short, hand-held hose like her mother used to use to bathe the dog.

There is a wonder here too. Beside the green ceramic counter, the refrigerator bulb glows near-fluorescent as the milk is transferred to the table. With the kitchen window shade left down the morning is muted, and they are already ready for the night to swallow them whole again. *Are we worthy?* he wonders, though worthy of what he does not ask himself. *Is this love?* she thinks, but does not want an answer from him.

The coffee is still filtering. She seems preoccupied with pushing down the ripples of her dark hair, hair like an old photograph, and he wonders what he will remember of her when he is actually old. He is shirtless, pulling on the day's first cigarette. His mouth, she notices, is like a small brown suckerfish amidst the dirty room. The room, crested with the thick smell of coffee, and half-filled with watery, algal silence.

THE PHYSICAL ACT OF LEAVING

THERE ARE VARYING depths of humiliation. Everything is relative.

We were dancing for the first time in several months. When people have birthdays, for whatever reason, they seem to feel this need to reclaim their youth. This ritual includes dragging their closest circle to atrocious bars, bopping to a strobe and sucking on long necks. In the deathly focus of the black light, blue teeth ghastly glowing...so attractive, I really can't relate.

On Leigh's last birthday she smoked too much dope and without any provocation threw herself in the river. It took three of us to fish her out, rush her home and hold her up in the shower to keep her from getting hypothermia. Afterwards she said it seemed as good a rebirth as any.

We don't intend to, she elaborated, but in the end we demean everyone by demeaning ourselves.

No wonder I was in love with her. Fucking drama queen.

Scared me right out of myself. But in retrospect, at least that year she didn't make us don club clothes, get sweaty alongside strangers, and drink a gallon of smoke. We had to save her from drowning, but we didn't have to clean up her vomit or anything like that. Why were her suicide attempts cleaner and less painful than the rest of her life?

It was about that time I realized that between the two of us our lives had begun to resemble a gay bar, a cast of mismatched characters parading about for strange, self-conscious spectacle. For whatever reason, I always felt like a majorette one step out of beat. Then again, I think Leigh felt that way too, even though she was always the one with the drum.

On this particular night, I began to notice the motion of age. Not the clothes or the haircuts, not even the nervous energy or false exuberance, but the way we each moved. I looked around the club and could peg people with a graduation year. I was stuck in some sort of semi-pogo dance myself. Others had that sports-bar shimmy with ultra ass emphasis, the long fingered flourishes of old goths, the kick-boxing motions of boys who'd been nineteen when Kurt Cobain killed himself, or the strange horse-clomping sneakers of rave kids. We were products of our time. How predictable, I thought.

And then, immediately, how predictable that I should think it.

We were dancing to a man and a woman on stage wearing black. They were both tall, with long black hair. Leigh leaned over and wondered aloud what he would be like to fuck. She was never the type to hold anything back. So I pointed out that the woman bassist was not so far from being a doo-wop girl, but damn, she did have stage presence. She would lean back, strumming slow and certain. He was literally on his knees, tooling around on his instrument. It was his show. His fingers were fast. His face contorted. He seemed, somehow, pathetic. But Leigh said she liked that.

The woman leaned back and tapped the strings: bom bom bombom. Just noise in a dark place. She was strangely aloof, serene. He looked like a baby in a tantrum—overindulgent and red-faced. Looking at the stage again, Leigh remarked that she didn't know who was more attractive.

Leigh had this urge to do him in the men's bathroom. She wanted my consent like a birthday present. She wanted it so much, she said it felt real, like it would happen. Like it already had.

That was when I think I knew that it was time to really leave her. That there was something wrong with her, something she couldn't stop if she tried. Everywhere she looked people were dancing for her. For her. I was her lover, but she wanted me to be the voyeur to her life. She was a grown woman and she acted like an eighteen-year-old boy.

I heard our friend Maggie once say that she has to come at least once a day. That makes me feel better about Leigh, that maybe she's not obsessed after all. I remember Leigh climbing on top of me at nineteen, begging me to make love to her, and I said no. I forget, was it No, I Can't? Or No, Not Now? Or just plain No? What kind of person says no? she asked me. I only remember her wanting like a choke-hold. Wanting like emerging from water into air. Wanting to climb to the top of me and swallow me. I know she wanted to but I didn't, and that's important. I didn't.

Maggie told Leigh we've all reached that age and she can't expect me to have the same kind of drive. Well, you didn't have it then, Leigh said, and I don't expect you to now.

But I knew we were still too young to be saying that we'd "reached that age" for anything.

I read an article in the newspaper about how we're sex obsessed as a culture and how ultimately it damages our enjoyment of the sexual act, because we are always considering its value. Like standing in a supermarket trying to decide between two brands of salsa and whether $1.99 will taste as good as $3.69, regretting the decision no matter which we choose. Thinking, damn, I shouldn't have blown all that money on groceries. Or shit, why didn't I buy the good kind? We are always comparing ourselves and our partners to some kind of perceived sexual standard. Did you come? Was it good for you? Is he good? Is she good? A repetitive paranoid sex pack mentality.

Leigh said, who's got time to comparison shop? Just grab one and go, it all tastes good.

Leigh also made a point of telling me that I was not the kind of person who goes over the edge. She never lies. It's true: I am the kind of person who ponders the edge. I run my toes along the rim; I test the temperature; I contemplate the dive.

The physical act of leaving.

I shove my face in the pillow and come as far as come is, but never actually go. Not the way she goes. Shivering, convulsing all over. Not the way other people describe going. Sailing away on the great surge of warmth as if the body were both heart and world. Me, everything just slowly stops; things leak out.

That is as much as I can give. Even as I am there with her, I imagine my body as that of the cartoon character who drinks water after a gun fight: the neat spouts seeping out in all directions from invisible holes. The human watering can. Plus motion. A grinding flour sifter that passes only the refined things through. Love and guts held in like tea leaves in a strainer. How do these images fill the brain when fucking?

Stop thinking so much, Leigh told me. Every time. It's not thinking, I responded. It's feeling. It must be, I tell myself, because I want to control it and can't. I wrote the words in a list on her back with my finger. This is how I feel:

Wanting—like a force beyond my control.

Wanting to leave my body and pass through.

Afraid to lose myself.

Afraid to leave her behind.

In the wake of my orgasm.

What if I leave my body and never come back? There are serious consequences to pleasure. I can do what I need to, but to let myself really get caught in the force of that action is something far more dangerous. I wouldn't think about it if I didn't have to. Believe me.

She didn't fuck that guy in the band. She didn't. But the impulse was there and she wasn't afraid to share it. Which is worse? The impulse or the honesty? For a long time I had this idea that if I could let myself really go with her just once, she would stop looking for someone else.

She'd met another guy, half a year earlier, that summer. A painter who had stopped painting. He said there was too much meaningless beauty. He said we were all trying to express one thing—just one—like a note of music, one note, one timbre. And that we would repeat it again and again in every gesture we ever made. Each of us has one note, he said. Just one.

That was all, according to Leigh, who relayed every word of her fantastic celibate affairs over our morning coffee. She dropped splintering bombs like that as easily as spoonfuls of sugar granules.

I saw it as unfair to him as to me. A cruelty so innocent it was beautiful. I no longer believed Leigh to be a sexual conqueror, more like a soul collector. She siphoned the essentials out of people quickly as fuel. Used them to get to herself. But ultimately, it meant she was bringing in the sounds and scents of hundreds of other people into our apartment. If not on her skin, then someplace inside her.

She licked her spoon and pulled at her bra strap until it untwisted with a snap. Said that was all I needed to know and that he was gone.

Do you forget that easily? I asked. I said his name to tease her. That night I traced it on her pillow with my finger, over her back, her breasts. I licked my palm to hold his tongue in my hand, my hand between her legs. I imagined him holding her face down into the pillow. The way he never would. The way I would never want. I pulled her hair with my other hand. And she smirked and squeaked and let me hold her down.

When I came I was him. Though I'd never seen it, I know I wore his face.

The bed was wet. I imagined his mouth and chin streaming with her scent.

But when she rolled over to face me, he was gone. It was just Leigh and me again.

She crossed her arms with one hand on each shoulder. She held herself. She cried with her teeth clamped shut—a high whinny of held back grief. That is the sound she made. The sound she makes.

She said her orgasm is just like being in the river, how when she finally got there, there was nothing. Not words. Not pleasure. Not pain. Waves like notes without names.

That was the problem. She wanted me to disappear and not be a person anymore. Become some shapeless tremoring thing. I could honey-mouth my way all over her, or I could humiliate her. It didn't make a lick of difference, as long as the attention was there. Negative, positive, they were the same. I entered into her, and she entered herself. Found a frequency I couldn't hear.

When Leigh hit the water, I went after her. Had the sense to throw off my winter coat before I vaulted the rail. Didn't even think about my shoes, the weight of them in water. Two seconds. That's all it took, from the parking lot across the grass and up and over and in. Two seconds. I don't know who it was who did it. It wasn't me. I remember only the car handle, and the dark. I went under the water in a half-dive, and when I came back up I could see her head for just a second as she thrust herself back under.

They say you shouldn't try to grab someone who can't swim, that they will pull you under with them.

But Leigh knew how to swim. So-so, like me. What she didn't know was how to drown. Drowning at will is not easy.

I don't remember what I said to her. Like I said, someone else was in the water with her. I was still in the parking lot with Neil and Maggie watching her heave herself over the railing.

I must have said the right thing, because she secured herself with a ridge of ice that was hanging from the guardwall, and she clung there while I shouted instructions and tried to find a way back out. When she realized that the wall was too high for me, and that Neil couldn't reach us even belly down with Maggie holding his ankles, Leigh started to panic. She hadn't thought of taking me with her.

How long did it take? Five minutes? Ten? Half my life. They were able to reach me first, and then I watched the six inches between Neil's fingers and Leigh's. A full hand's length away growing longer. There was an awful moment when I saw her fading back into the water.

Neil yelled my name, twice, even though I was right there. I'm losing her, he said. To me, not to her, almost as if she were already gone.

A moment of decision, maybe, and then she ducked, found a footing on the rusted wall, and sprang up, catching him by his last knuckle.

All the way home in the car she screamed at the top of her lungs, and Maggie thought we needed to take her to the hospital. At the apartment Leigh wouldn't let Neil undress her even though I was frantically trying to untangle myself from my own clothes.

As I held her against me in the hot shower blast, she came back into herself. What took you so fucking long? she laughed. Her forehead fell against my chest, her mouth against my nipple and she kissed it like a consolation prize while she shook and cried.

Not long after the painter she'd met an ex-punk photographer. He'd heard about her river stint and wanted her to pose wrapped in fishing line with lures instead of clit or nipples. Leigh thought it was a hilarious metaphor for her life and came away with marks all over her.

And then there were girls, though they scared me less because I knew they wouldn't cross the line. But still I could hear their laughter ringing in Leigh's ears when she walked through the door. It was like it was dripping onto our pillow, and their voices were filling my head at night.

I came up with a title for a poem I was meaning to write for Leigh. It was called, "There Will Always Be Someone Else." I said this line to myself over and over to convince myself not to worry about her crushes, the incompetent sense of possession flitting through me, the fear of our going over the edge.

It is not important, I said, it is normal and not worth worrying about these distractions. I tried to write the next line—in order to make each new person generic. To line them up side by side, quietly order them into submission. To forget them and ignore them. Give her back to me in my mind.

"There will always be someone else," I wrote at the tops of blank pages. "There will always be someone else." It became an assignment, a set of lines I gave myself for her naughty behaviour.

I was too old for this ritual. A song with the verses indistinguishable from the chorus. Noise in a dark place.

I repeated the same words again and again until they sounded like a foreign language, and I still could not write the rest. This poem for Leigh, nothing but a strange note to myself.

I bobbed in the white noise of another kind of river. Without ever making my own jump, I had left myself. To find nothing left, but myself.

THE VALUE OF X

IF ANYONE KNEW what kind of girl Jeanette (henceforth represented by J.) really was, they would have strung her from the flagpole of the school, J. was certain. She didn't know when it started. One day she was just casually looking around the classroom at the boys, and the next thing she knew all the boys had become girls. Of course no one else noticed but J. It was sort of her special secret power. To transform men with her eyes. Like Superman and his X-ray vision...no one else knew what she saw. J. had XY-to-XX vision.

And later, much later, she would hone her power and develop XX-to-XY vision as well.

She couldn't be certain of the exact moment of time, but it seemed as though it might have begun with Eric Gunnarman and the Cocoa Transparent. Cocoa Transparent (as opposed to Cocoa Creme) was J.'s favourite lipstick that year. Meanwhile, Eric Gunnarman sat across from J. for two semesters, unsuspectingly turning his one small gold earring and tapping his pencil on his math book, not thinking at all about the value of x. While he was leaning back in his chair, chest far too broad for a ninth grade boy...J. was mentally drawing breasts over his semi-developed pecks and applying Cocoa Transparent to his chubby, pale boy-lips.

This is perfect, J. thought to herself. *This is the perfect, perfect colour. Not just for Eric, but for everyone.* J. herself was entering her second season of Cocoa Transparent, and had already coaxed a tube onto her best friend, Marnie. Marnie was a redhead; J. was brunette; and Angie (Marnie's older sister) was a natural blonde...and had stolen the Cocoa Transparent in Marnie's third week, refusing to give it back because Angie insisted it was the perfect colour for a blonde/brown such as herself. *And now*, thought J., *this*. Eric Gunnarman, blonde/blue and more stubble than any other four-teen-year-old hopeful. *And still*, thought J., *still...Cocoa Transparent fits*. It was a revelation.

Perhaps it was at this point J.'s mission swung into full force, as she began drawing lipstick and eventually eyeliner, mascara and blush onto the boys in band, the junior boys' volleyball team, and even Mr. Henry, the sixty-year-old custodian whose sunken gentle eyes could only be truly appreciated when viewed with a fine sheen of Silver Mist eyeshadow (at the corners, of course, not over the whole lid).

But when J. met Zachary Saunderson (henceforth represented by Z.), everything changed. And perhaps, it was then, that she really began to use her super powers for some purpose. She was sitting on the bleachers during assembly one sweaty September just days into tenth grade, when she saw him. All the way from across the auditorium. She looked at him and he looked at her, and she knew...Cocoa Transparent would simply never do.

Z. was leaning against the back door of the gymnasium, long black shirt untucked, hands stuck in pockets, shoulders balled forward as though the gym wall was collapsing on his back and pushing them forward. Black hair ragged over one eye, the other fixed on her, almost as if...he knew. He knew what she was doing, gazing flippantly up and down the rows, her quirky mouth drawn into a concentrated, crude half-smile. He knew that she was browning up the lips of pure, innocent, unsuspecting boys with her secret, queer, filthy mind. Oh yes, Z. knew. She looked at Z. from beneath her perfectly gelled, perfectly curled, perfect pretence forehead and Z. looked at her from beneath his unkempt bangs, untucked shirt, and uncut candour and she knew he knew what she had been up to. And why.

Why? It was then that J. panicked. J. didn't love boys at all. All those after-school flirtations with Brian Anderson and Dave McGee at drama rehearsals were only feeble attempts to see if they would allow her to do their makeup backstage before performance. To see if they might allow her to transform them into...girls. *Girls*, J. thought with shock. *Girls!* The whole time she had been flirting with boys, she had been flirting with girls. It was only girls that she could truly adore.

J. ran gagging from the gymnasium.

In the bathroom, she spit in the sink, and washed the remaining residue of Cocoa Transparent from her lips. She was a liar. She, J., Super Girl Transformer of Faces and Souls was a liar. She looked at herself in the murky mirror, her dark image reflected like a mug shot with the high school-green/hospital-green wall as a backdrop. That's where she belonged. In a hospital for girls who did perverted things (like turning boys into girls), all the while pretending they were straight students—straight-A with nice manners and clean fingernails, who would grow up to be nice, responsible members of society. No. She was not. She would not. She was a liar. Her super powers were useless in the face of this realization. She had been using her powers for evil.

She looked at herself: her hair slicked back with water, her face stark without lipstick, blush, eyeliner...she was uncovered. Her secret identity secret from herself. Now exposed. J. was a boy. *This explains everything,* she screamed silently at the mirror. *You lousy bastard. Only a man would put me through this. I should have known you were a boy all along, to act this way, to string me along and put me through this.*

At that moment J.'s best friend Marnie came into the bathroom to see if J. was all right.

I'm so embarrassed, J. confided.

Why? What happened? Marnie put her arm around J.

All this time I've been wearing that lipstick, J. said. *How could I not have known? How could I not have known?* she wailed, cringing into Marnie's open arms.

Marnie, like a good friend, took heed of J.'s confession, and relegated Cocoa Transparent to a long list of last year's trends. She wiped her own mouth immediately as if it would solve everything. And again, without quite meaning to, J. had made another transformation.

Z. Saunderson was waiting near J.'s locker after fourth period. His wrinkled shirt hung so far from his thin frame that it may as well have been a child's Halloween cape.

What do you want? J. asked him. It was the first thing she had ever said to him, and she banged her locker door open as if to punctuate herself.

I thought—I thought—I thought—he stuttered, so quickly he seemed to be cutting himself off.

You don't think; you know, J. said. And with that she banged the locker door closed. This was the beginning of their strange affinity, punctuated by abrupt banging sounds, and opening and closing. It went unsaid that he should follow her out of the school, and across the student parking lot, and up to the patch of grass behind the tennis courts where they could sit on the picnic table and not smoke (as neither of them were smokers) and not talk (as neither of them were really talkers), and not drink Coke or Pepsi (as neither one of them had any particular alliance with either corporation, nor any money for the purchase, nor any forethought of this meeting). It went without saying that Z. was neither an XX or an XY, he was a small x. The small x in J.'s grand plan, the unknown factor she felt she had to isolate in order to prove its worth.

Red, said J.

Red? said Z.

Not just red, J. said, Crimson.

Constant Crimson. Z. turned the tube over in his hand to look at the butt end of it where the wrapper indicated its type, its colour, number and name.

In J.'s bedroom Z. was a red-hot firecracker, a pure explosion of good and evil rolled into one. All bang and fantastic spraying light. He lay back on her bed kicking his feet. He did headstands on the pillows. He lipsync-ed to Prince's "Little Red Corvette" and The The's "I've Been Waiting For Tomorrow (All Of My Life)." He rearranged the books on J.'s shelves by publication date.

The night after she got her driver's licence, she took him out to Dead Fuck Hill, aptly nicknamed because as the one and only hill in town (a mammoth man-made breast bulging out of flat earth) it was also one of the few places where kids could get stoned or drunk out of sight of the street. J. and Z. stood on the hill together and didn't touch. Again they had brought nothing with them (as neither of them were either drinkers or smokers, still after all these eight months since their first rendezvous). They stood and they stared at the sky and they didn't point out stars because it was too dark and there were too many clouds. So they just stood. Together. And didn't touch.

What are we doing here? Z. asked eventually.

I thought I would bring you here so I could listen to you breathe, J. said. And she meant it.

The field was quiet except for a few crickets farther over near the fence and the ungrown cornfield behind it. The town was a tinkly trail of light-specs and occasional car-honks, but with that exception, the field and the sky were swelling together with silence.

Z. plugged his nose, and held out for as long as he could. Then he ran screaming down the side of the hill, *I am a stereotype of myself.*

It was better that way, J. knew. Things were getting too serious. She was the one making them serious. But eventually they would have to define. Was she really XX or XY? Were they friends? Were they boyfriend and girl-friend? *What?* The friends J. still had, like Marnie, were beginning to ask embarrassing questions in far-too-public places, as if these things were just the usual-goings-on. People J. no longer considered friends, or who never had been friends, leaned out of lockers to whisper and snicker as she and Z. walked by holding hands, *practising*, Z. said, for the spring musical, some-times going so far as to sing "People Will Say We're In Love." It was all a joke to Z. A big, luscious, juicy joke he could sink his teeth into and spit out in their faces. *Am I part of that joke?* J. wondered sometimes.

But for now, she told herself, *it's better this way*. Because J. still didn't know. That day in the auditorium, she had felt transparent when Z. looked at her. She had known she did not like boys. But then...she had gotten to know Z. And he was neither a boy nor a girl. In her humble opinion. In her humble, not-so-Super-J.-Girl opinion. And she was neither a girl nor a boy. And so they seemed...matched.

So when he didn't take his cue and kiss her on Dead Fuck Hill, J. recharged her XX-XY powers, and bought him the Constant Crimson lipstick.

Z. was enamoured with her gift. He rolled the silver tube back and forth between his fingers as if it were a thing of great value. Or, maybe, J. thought as he turned it end over end, a sexual instrument. Z. was suddenly shy.

Do you want it? J. asked him. *Because I didn't want to presume...I mean, if you don't, it's okay.*

Of course I want it, he said. *I just didn't know I wanted it. I wouldn't have bought it for myself. I would have been too scared.* Z. smiled. *I wouldn't have had the balls*, he added with a straight face.

Come on then, J. said, spurred on by his good nature, *I'll put it on you.* (In retrospect, perhaps that was going a bit too far, J. would think, knowing herself and her motives as well as she did.)

Z.'s lips were the plush carpet of lips. Z.'s lips were to-die-for. They were thick lips that demanded to be lounged on, with a cushiony top lip that covered a rough, sexy overbite...and a bottom lip that sunk in as if it was sulking and hiding from the pretty top one.

J. treaded very softly on them with the colour held steady in her right hand, and J.'s chin held carefully in her left. She reddened him. The full top lip first. And then the scared bottom.

When she held the mirror up, she watched Z.'s face for some sign. His slowest smile. His reddest red. His happiest happy.

Then she knew. What he knew. She knew.

Here faggot faggot, she would call to him in the hallway at school. *Here faggot. Good boy. Sit. Stay.* And he would sit at her feet and pretend to pant.

It was a terrible joke but he loved it. More than she did. *Because*, he said, *because...they can't beat it.*

It was true. No one bothered J. or Z. No one leaned out of lockers to snicker or whisper anymore. No one dared. Between the two of them, they had pooled their super powers. They had become all powerful. They had claimed their secret identities as their own. They had defined.

Z. was XX. J. was XY.

In public. In private, neither J. nor Z. knew quite what they were.

Here faggot faggot, she called him from her perch on the dresser.

No, you come here, faggot, he called her from the bed.

Then they would wrestle. *Ding ding*, she would yell out and they would break to lie with their arms around each other and she would kiss his Constant Crimson lips which he now kept constantly crimson. She would kiss him until the crimson came off and stained her face like blood. Then he would yell *ding ding*, and round two would begin, with him shrieking wildly and her giggling and grunting, trying to pin him.

Say Uncle, Z. would holler, folding her in half.

Auntie, J. would spit up at him. Her only punchline. Only funny because it was so obvious, so given.

Z.'s punchlines were always more clever, more abstract, harder sometimes with a truth that took time before it could be seen through its subtlety.

What J. didn't tell Z. was that she had already established a few very clear rules in her head for their behaviour, the paths she would and would not allow. It was obvious to her that one day they would leave one another. Z. was a year older, so it stood to reason that he would leave first. Granted, J. did better in school, so it might come to be that they would both leave at the same time. Still...J. assumed that even if they left for the same places, they would wind up going in different directions. J. didn't know if she liked girls. She had never kissed one yet after all this time. Small town and all. Not many opportunities. But she liked girlish boys. This was obvious.

And Z. obviously liked boyish girls as well as girlish girls (which J. fully represented in the physical sense with or without her lipstick), and girlish boys and boyish boys too if he could have ever gotten his hands on any.

What they had was temporary, J. was quite certain. She could see no other answer. Move out, go to university, live together, get married, work, buy house, have kids, die. This sequence of events was improbable. J. was already working ahead to include two twelfth-grade-level maths, and knew all about calculating probability.

These are the kinds of things J. wrote down on scrap pieces of paper that did not constitute any kind of a diary, but more like an ongoing series of rough note pages. The kind of scratch pad that does not make sense to someone else who has meandered along and happened upon it...a series of numbers or letters without meaning attached to them. A missing component. A coded language.

J. wrote: *boy girl girl boy girl girl boy boy girl boy us kids*.

J. wrote: *no*.

J. wrote: *yes*.

J. wrote: *love = sex ?*

J. wrote: *2, 6, 3, 1* (which stood for years, months, weeks, days together)

J. wrote: *1, 8, 2, 5* (which stood for years, months, weeks, days 'til Z.'s graduation)

J. wrote: *Point?*

J. wrote: *Counterpoint* (in spite of the fact that she had not yet written the point with any clarity).

It was ridiculous. All of it. J. made each of these entries on separate pages. She kept the book in an obvious place, the top drawer of her dresser, because she was certain no one who looked for it or read it would understand her thoughts anyway. She wrote in the book rarely, but the entries were always alike.

One of the rules that was fixed clearly in J.'s mind (and which she did not ever write down explicitly) was that she would not have sex with Z. unless he let her have sex with him. To be more precise, J. had decided that she would not let Z. enter her body unless she was allowed to enter his. *Fair is fair,* J. told herself. And, she admitted to herself it sounded a bit harsh. But J. was never interested in sacrificing herself to Z. She was interested in sharing. Because, above all, they were friends. *Share and share alike.*

It was Christmas Eve. J. was seventeen. Z. came over with a loaf of date bread for J.'s mother and father. J.'s mother adored Z. and greeted him at the door with dish-soap hands and cheek kisses. J.'s father never said anything and J. interpreted his silences as, *Why don't you get yourself a real boyfriend and stop dating this freak?* though such things were never stated even covertly in households as nice as J.'s (with parents who were such good, responsible citizens with such nice manners and clean fingernails). J.'s dad looked up and said, *Oh date bread*, and then continued programming the VCR.

J.'s bedframe was wrapped with strings of red and white lights. *What's this for?* Z. asked.

I wanted to give you something that wasn't a physical, material object, J. said. All day she thought about what she would say, but these weren't quite the words and now it sounded blunt. *Something tangible, but intangible, that can't be kept.* She realizes now it is even blunter.

Z. was nervous and kept giggling and shushing and pushing J. away. Not just because J.'s parents were downstairs. They were downstairs during all of J. and Z.'s improvised WWF afternoons. That night, Z. made jokes about J.'s mother in the kitchen, stuffing the bird for the next day, reaching a gloved hand into its hollow parts in the room directly below where they were now...just as they were...

J. thought, *Shut up...I love you*. J. said, *Shut up and let me*. She felt like she was forcing him, though she knew that he wanted to do it too. She steered him into a kneeling position over top of her. He resisted her at first and then he took her in. He was warm. His body felt burning hot inside. His eyes were wide open, terrified for a second. He came almost instantly across her stomach, his blank eyes floating in the darkness like white unattached stars, his mouth open. He gasped once and lurched and then the liquid fell out of him. It felt like everything inside his thin body had spilled out and he collapsed on her shoulder as if he was dead.

After her hurried-finger turn, they stood together naked in front of her mirror. J. tousled Z.'s hair back into disorder and put his lipstick on for him.

I think you really are a gay man, Z. remarked, deadpan. He straightened his shoulders. *Do you like the way I look?* he asked.

I love the way you look. You look like you. J. said. But she never said I love you. She didn't think of it at the time. She thinks of it now.

The heart is far enough removed from the head, far enough to be less personal somehow, to hold less fear. J. assumes that is why Z. chose his heart, though it would not have been the most secure way.

J. remembers that night as the last time she saw him, though it wasn't. She thinks of the sticky, silver trail he shot across her that was hot like wax. How he was like a star burning out. How he shook, terrified. How she touched him inside, in the core of his body. How everything inside him fell out on her.

One minute everything inside him was blasting warm on her skin. And the next minute he was dead. That is not how it happened. There was time between. Time that was passed in the same ways as always, time that left no clues. But what J. remembers is that night as the last. She remembers it as a kind of evidence. That Z. was. What Z. was. When she was inside him. When he was inside her.

Z.'s heart was what he chose to shoot. Four weeks after the night in J.'s bed. On his eighteenth birthday with his father's police pistol. He was found in a cornfield about five kilometres from Dead Fuck Hill. J. was glad it wasn't at the Hill. She wouldn't have known how to interpret that. She wouldn't have had the right codes.

What J. thought was that what they were doing, acting like the Wonder Twins, running around transforming themselves into buckets of water and whatnot, was temporary. It was ecstatic. *Ecstatic things are about moment*, J. wrote on her note pad. And after their Christmas Eve, J. wrote: *Enter. Love. Z. cried.*

There are entries that cover the weeks that J. doesn't remember. They are the usual kind of entries J. made, smugness and insecurity stacked back to back, one side of the page and the other.

J. wrote: *Someday. See Z. on street. Say hi.*

J. wrote: *Girlfriend will ask about him. Sing 'My own personal drag queen' to tune of Depeche Mode's "Personal Jesus."*

J. wrote: *I = Z. Z.= me*

J. wrote: *Now.*

J. wrote: *Later?*

J. wrote: *1, 6, 3, 1*

J. wrote: *Take Z. to Hill again this spring. Make listen.*

What J. never wrote were the things that were outside of their relationship, the things she had no control over. Z.'s angry alcoholic father tearing down Z.'s posters and throwing out his comics, constantly telling him to grow up and make decisions in his life. Z.'s mother who only baked and sulked. Z.'s grades that plunged in direct relation to his soaring antics. His occasional cruelty. His consistent sadness. His jokes pulled from the belt of gadgets that held his pants up.

In retrospect J. saw their relationship as the only thing that was not temporary, as the only thing either of them really had that could hold them to the world. Super J. with her super powers, her XX-XY vision, transforming Z. into various personages and objects to distract him from himself. She-heroes and nemeses.

J. saw herself drawing faces onto Z., and Z. drawing sideburns onto her. Twins, outfitted in purple, standing with hands on hips ready to fight for truth, justice. Their world a sad satire of itself. J. saw herself pouring Z. out of himself, frivolously, like a joke. A bucket of water secured above some door that he himself would open. Inside the bucket, all the things she couldn't name.

J. insisted on not taking time off school. She wore Z.'s Constant Crimson for courage. People stared at her like she was the dead one.

J. told her mother she knew this was going to happen. J. told Z.'s mother she knew. J. told everyone that *though* she didn't know, she still *knew*. J. said it again and again. She said it because she didn't know. She didn't know why he didn't tell her.

It goes without saying, that she felt it was her fault. That she had pulled off his costume—transformed him into a foreign shape for which he wasn't equipped. And as it goes without saying, J. avoided saying any such thing.

Instead, seized by a morbid sense of humour on the day of the funeral, J. wore Z.'s Pixies' *Death to the Pixies* concert shirt and seriously considered that Z. might be haunting her.

She had a desire to buy firecrackers to set off on the grave. With Z. isolated on the other side, super powers or none, it seemed the only signal of celebration for his life that she could draw on. But as it was still February, and firecrackers never sold until May, she abandoned the plan shortly after breakfast.

At the funeral home, J. proposed sitting in the back row, as if Z. were a stranger to her, instead of her friend, her lover. *Everything is ludicrous*, J. thought, imagined that Z. might sit up halfway through the service with another punchline for the funeral director. Or for her. The unpredicted act of death, his final punchline. J. laughed a hiccup of a laugh. She had a terrible feeling that Z. *would* very much like her to sit in the back row and laugh long peeling trills, as if he were up in front of an audience standing on his head. J. put her head down and continued to hiccup-laugh. Her mother gave her a strange, sharp look.

The long white room felt like a box, the cold decor carefully chosen for its anonymity. J. suddenly became claustrophobic, sitting there in Z.'s clothing and lipstick, shoulders bowled, as if she had become him, two rows away from the body that the mortician had drained the fluids from and replaced with formaldehyde. To keep him. To preserve him. *Where are his fluids now?* J. wondered. *Did they throw them out? Flush them away?* Her breath snagged in her chest, jiggling inside of her like a latch that wouldn't undo.

J. could picture Z. doing the research for this, the best angle to shoot so as not to make a mess of everything for everyone else. That's why the heart. It would require a steadier hand...easier to slip at the last minute, try to pull oneself away, hit the lung. Greater chance for failure, but less direct fear, the coldness of the gun's mouth through clothing instead of within one's peripheral vision, pressed directly to the temple...or the more obvious gun-in-mouth tactic and the phallic insinuations others might make, not right away of course, but later, at parties or at the Hill. To shoot into the chest would leave less physical damage to the body. J. assumed, knowing Z., he probably thought of it just like that, matter-of-factly, like any other thing, on a trip to the tiny town library. The open casket for closure.

When she went up to stand over the body, J. realized Z. was not represented as Z. His hair was neatly sculpted. A black suit with a vest had been chosen to cover the wounds. His shoulders...flat and straight on the pillow as if he had at last unfolded from himself. Z.'s hands closed over the place his heart once was. The mortician had covered him in a far too dark foundation as if to compensate for Z.'s unusually pale complexion. J. wondered if it was beyond a mortician to think that someone who looked dead in life should look dead in death. If J. didn't know Z. she would have thought he was a nice responsible member of society with good manners and clean fingernails. Death had smoothed Z. over with slight pale pinks around his eyes; his lips, Absolutely Peach.

J. drew her breath in, listened to it over top of all the other minute sounds in the room.

J. wanted to kiss Z.'s entire face, to smear him with red, to leave him Constant Crimson, as he did her so many times in her bed. It would seem, somehow, more fitting than this.

Instead she took a deep breath and called on Super J. who came swooping down from the ceiling to save her and avenge. J. took Z.'s lipstick from her pants' pocket and, without touching Z. with her hands, she drew the lines of his mouth by memory, tracing the full upper lip slowly. She had applied his lipstick so often, the shape was obvious to her as her own mouth, a mouth she could put lipstick on without a mirror, without eyesight or touch.

He wouldn't have liked those faggy colours.

WHAT IS SARAH CHATEL THINKING?

WHAT DOES SHE think about when he fucks her? That's what I wonder when Mr. Peck takes attendance and Sarah Chatel thumbs little sparkly silver heart stickers onto the back of her boyfriend Jay's jean jacket. *What does she think about when he fucks her?*

Sarah Chatel is the one girl in our town who has already done something—professional modelling. She's also on the volleyball team and the swim team, and she's an Honours student. I imagine she must not think of anything, but I can't imagine how she can do it. Clear her brain of everything for the whole twelve minutes it must take. *Twelve minutes*, I think, *twelve minutes times sixty seconds...* I assure myself I'm paying attention as Mr. Peck takes up the math homework... *Twelve times sixty is...a long time when you are lying in one position not really doing anything.*

Jay turns around and grunts at her, Cut it out hey. Can't you see I'm trying to get this?

Jay has no interest in math. It's a joke. He knows and she knows that if he gets too close to failing, she will help him.

I imagine the two of them up in the dressing room behind the stage. How Aaron Dixon walked in on them last Friday night during the school dance to try to retrieve the forty of vodka he'd stashed there earlier. How he passed the story around the whole gym by the time the night was over: Sarah Chatel with her legs over Jay Johnson's shoulders, and her eyes rolled back into her head. The future prom queen finally deflowered two years before the grade twelve formal.

Way to go Jay, the guys said slapping him on the shoulder as he left the dance. You're the man, Johnson.

I saw Sarah Chatel at that dance. Beforehand, I think. I'm pretty sure it must have been before. She wasn't drunk or anything. She never is. She was in the girls' bathroom with Janet Lafontaine and Rae Ann DuChene like she always is. They were ice queens as usual. Too cool to fight for a spot at the mirror, for fixing hair or pencilling new eyeliner. Too cool to talk to anyone, including each other. They were sitting around by the showers mostly just looking at each other and away, once in a while saying cryptic things, like, Well what do you expect? And, If you're like that you know it's going to be like that, and strange in-jokes which left them smirking, phrases like Join the Club, Pocket Protector, and okay, maybe even Kahoona. In retrospect, the Get-Ready-to-Crack-the-Big-V conversation to a T. But at the time, I didn't want to believe that Sarah Chatel was letting Jay Johnson pound it into her not thirty feet from where the rest of us were desperately trying to find dance partners for Led Zeppelin's "Stairway to Heaven."

But now that I'm sitting here in Peck's math class, and Sarah is drawing one mauve fingernail up and down the back of Jay Johnson's big brown head, it is really obvious that she let him do just that on Friday and that she will let him do it again. Do her. Screw her. Nail her. Ball her. Bang her. Bam her. Ram her. Take her. Make her. Fuck her. *It's like a poem*, I think, and I'm still thinking in Mrs. Hine's English class, *like a poem*:

> Do her
> Screw her Nail her
> Ball her Bang her Bam her Ram her
> Take her Make her
> Fuck her

I consider writing it down and handing it in at the end of class. I don't, but I sing it in my head while walking home until Sasha gets fed up with me and asks if I'm listening to a word she's said. And I am. I am listening: Mr. Peters doesn't understand—*Do her Screw her*—how hard it is—*Nail her*—when I can't see the blackboard— *Ball her Bang her Ram her Bam her*—I wish he would just let me sit at the front—*Take her Make her*—by the windows, are you listening to me?—*Fuck her.*

Sasha lends me a V.C. Andrews novel, which, even when I take, I'm certain is absolute crap, but I skim it that night for the good parts. The parts where the brother and sister don't know what to do about their blossoming adulthood and how confused she is by her pubic hair, and how he can't help it, he just can't help it...

I lie in bed with the lights off not thinking of Jay Johnson. What I should be thinking of, I tell myself, is Jay Johnson. I try to make myself think of him with his shirt off like he always is after basketball practice. I try to imagine the small wiry circles of black hair around his nipples or the perfectly hairless six-pack stomach he achieved since he turned sixteen and was able to get membership to the gym. I try to imagine him pulling down my shorts and underwear in one quick motion, and me pulling his jeans down with an almost shy, coy wince. I try to imagine his cock in my hand. But in my mind, the thing is dirty and huge and shapeless, like a big loud smear of mustard on the night. I try to imagine the texture, the colour and shape. The balls. The hair. The head. I get them in the wrong order. Upside down. They seem misplaced, like a biology class diagram on LSD. So I try again. I whisper it into my pillow. Cock. Cock. Again and again. Cock cock cock. Fuck me with your cock, I say as Jay Johnson tries to find a way into me with his big balloon-shaped dick and tennis-ball balls, desperately ready to spill my virginal blood all over the hardwood floor of the shadowy stage room as the opening chords of "Stairway to Heaven" reverberate backwards from the speakers on the other side of the drywall.

And as I put my finger inside myself, I find myself looking up at the cracked dark of my own bedroom ceiling. And I realize that if Jay Johnson was here, over top of me right now, my eyes would probably be crushed into his shoulder so I could barely breathe—his shoulder that is still covered in acne. In spite of everything else. And his head would be lumbering around someplace over top of mine, because he's so tall. And his armpits would be near my nose. And even though I really shouldn't, I stop trying to think of

Jay Johnson. I turn over into my pillow and I think of Sarah Chatel. I imagine her lying there underneath him—and then underneath me—just like this pillow, motionless, waiting.

Stupid cunt, I swear at myself for thinking of it.

Very slowly, very quietly so my mom and dad won't know I am still awake, I get up and fumble carefully over to my dresser where I have a hand-held mirror and a flashlight. Back in bed, quietly under the covers, I prop myself up on my hands and knees and position the mirror underneath me. With the flashlight on top of the pillow I can see nearly everything, if I can manage to stay at a certain angle in the beam. I begin again, hesitantly thumbing down white underpants, listening intently for noises outside the room.

Sarah Chatel is an open pink apparition beneath me, her body distinct, lit up, alive like a thing that has been lived in, a seashell-like ear for hearing the ocean, a pursed wet purple mouth.

I imagine what she might have said or might not have said as she was undressed slowly, each white button on her black blouse a sugar cube in the dark, clicking against teeth and fingernails. She says, *Oh, oh, oh.* She says, *Don't tell anyone.* She says, *Who do you think you are?* She says, *No, please don't.* She says, *Yes, yes.* She says, *I've never done this before.* She says, *Do you love me?* She says, *I love you.* She says, *Maybe.*

She does not say, *Fuck me with your big hard cock. I want to feel you slide deep inside. I want you to Do me Screw me Nail me Ball me Bang me Bam me Ram me Take me Make me Fuck me.*

She is not like me. She does not lie awake at night breathing bad words into her pillow, trying to make herself think of things. She just does things. She does not have to think about them.

Tuesday morning in Pecker's math class, Sarah Chatel is writing notes to Jay Johnson with a baby blue felt-tip pen. The round bubble-letters make me think of the bubble-gum penis I imagined last night and, to keep myself from looking at either of them, I draw tight little lines in pencil around the holes in the margin of my notebook.

In Hiney's English class the margin of my notebook looks like a whole beach of seashells, and I draw red waves along the top of the page to underline the date: Tuesday, September 16. *Monday's child is fair of face, Tuesday's child is full of grace*, I sing in my head. I think about writing down my fantasy from last night and handing it in for creative writing assignment. I think about it for all of half a second. Twelve minutes divided by sixty seconds divided by one second divided in half. That is how little I think of either Sarah Chatel or Jay Johnson on Tuesday.

On Wednesday morning, Jay Johnson brings a friendship bracelet for Sarah, and slips it to her just before Pecker collects the homework. Jay starts humming Van Halen's "When It's Love", and it occurs to me for the first time that maybe *she* popped *his* cherry. Sarah smiles like she's embarrassed, and pokes the bracelet into her pencil case instead of putting it on.

During afternoon break, outside the cafeteria, Sarah Chatel calls Jay Johnson a Useless Prick. I imagine he has broken some kind of unspoken rule about forming attachments too quickly. He looks devastated as she walks away, as though he might cry, but he maintains face by banging his fist against the locker instead. Useless Prick, I write carefully and mischievously on the inside back page of my English notebook during Hiney's class.

That night at home, I say it over and over to myself as I fall asleep. Useless Prick. Useless Prick. Useless Prick. I'm titillated by the phrase—the idea that it has streamed out of Sarah Chatel's little violet-lipsticked mouth in the middle of a crowded hallway. I imagine her saying it to Jay Johnson alone backstage as he struggles to get it up. I imagine him slapping himself around trying to get it going, and in the end all he can manage are two tear-sized drops of semen that land on Sarah's left calf before he can get anywhere near her vagina. His cum is thin, like milk. Useless Prick, she tells him, and I cum all over the thought of her. In my head I think of it like that anyway, though I'm not sure if women are technically supposed to "cum." In my head it is "cum." But inside me it is an ocean.

On Thursday I am full of guilt, as Jay Johnson slinks into Peck's class late and hunches down in his seat without looking at anyone. I feel sorry for him, because, I tell myself, he really isn't that bad. Not like the hockey guys. And what did he ever do to Sarah Chatel besides like her? Sarah Chatel draws droopy daisies with a fat pink highlighter. She smiles at me when she sees me glancing over. I feel even guiltier as I smile back.

By lunchtime, Sarah's best friends, Janet Lafontaine and Rae Ann DuChene have stopped speaking to her, and are sitting at a table with Jay Johnson and Aaron Dixon and three other guys from basketball. I am sitting with Sasha, and Monica and Nicole from band. They are giving each other a quiz from a magazine. The quiz is called, "The Best Language is Body Language: What Are You Telling Him?" Though one of the sweetest people I've ever met, Nicole has a uni-brow and got her first kiss this summer from her thirteen-year-old brother's best friend. Monica wins the science award every year, but is painfully shy and a tad overweight. It turns out Nicole is Class D-Desperate and Monica is Class A-Aggressive. Considering they hardly speak to anybody but each other it seems hardly likely, Sasha interjects, and I almost wish I'd thought of it, though of course, I wouldn't have actually said it. I'm just about to take the quiz when Sarah Chatel sits down next to me.

Do you want to take the quiz? Sasha offers Sarah.

I could kill Sasha. Doesn't she think, I wonder. Isn't it obvious that Sarah just broke up with someone and probably doesn't care what kind of body language she gives?

To my surprise, Sarah agrees, and pulls a pale pink bologna sandwich from her brown bag. I notice the squirts of mustard that have soaked to the edges of the white bread. I notice she has decals of monarch butterflies on her mauve fingernails. New since this morning. She is wearing a rusty lipstick too, which is a switch for her, and I have this suspicion that she skipped second period to go shopping and console herself. I watch the way she bites real-sized bites and not delicate model-girl bites out of the sandwich. I notice when she smears her fingers on her perfect form-fitting jeans, and scratches at her ponytail unconsciously in a way that makes her hair scrunch up into that Nearly-Perfect-but-Just-Natural-Enough way. I memorize all her answers:

1. b) she likes to look people in the eyes
2. a) she likes touching people when she talks to them
3. a) she sometimes feels like she talks too loud
4. c) she walks with her head down
5. d) she finds she is more animated when she talks to boys than girls
6. c) she likes to lean against walls and counters
7. b) she never says yes when she means no—regardless of the situation (several situations suggested in the three parts of question 7)
8. b) she plays sports or performs
9. b) she has a good memory for names
10. b) in a dating situation she would use both physical cues and spoken language to communicate her intentions and desires.

Of course, she is Class B-Best Chance of Getting the Boy Without Compromising. Of course, it's obvious that you're supposed to pick all Bs, but she humours us and says that she really thought she was more of a Class C-Confused signals. Of course, when Sasha wants me to take the quiz I don't. I know that if I answer honestly I will be a Class C-Confused signals, and if I don't answer honestly Sasha (who is probably Class A-Aggressive) will yell out that I am *so lying*. Instead, I try to look cool and bored. I try not to think about whatever Sarah Chatel might think of us. I pull out my notebook and cover it in doodles with my black ballpoint.

I like your seashells, Sarah says in that misty voice of hers, and I feel the back of my head get hot as if I've been sitting in the sun. I can't help but bend my face down under the weight of her eyes, even though I'm nearly certain the seashells don't look to her like what they are to me.

Thanks, I say and close the book.

And I already know that when I go home tonight I will be way beyond my feeble attempts to think of Jay Johnson. I know that I will replay all of Sarah's answers like a song in my head, especially that last one about her intentions and desires, and I'll imagine her saying, *I like your seashells, I like your seashells*, over and over again as the little monarch butterflies flutter by. And this time while I imagine Jay Johnson fucking her in the dressing room, she won't be thinking about Jay Johnson at all. Or even about fucking. I will imagine that she goes far, far away from Jay, to a place in her head full of diamond sand dunes and purple waves that suck at the pebbles along the waterline. And all Jay will think about is how he has to concentrate very hard because he doesn't want to cum yet. He will be thinking about the way his dick forces her open. And he will believe that she too, is imagining the way it must look down there when his dick forces her open. He will have no idea where she really is or what she is thinking.

And I'll think of the blobby mustard on her sandwich and her wiping her fingers on her jeans and calling Jay Johnson a Useless Prick, and I'll know what I already know...that I'm like Jay Johnson, the person who likes her too much to really see her or be her. And I'll never know what she thinks when she fucks. Or what she thinks about anything. Period.

By Friday, Sarah Chatel and Jay Johnson are back together. By the time Mr. Peck has explained the difference between square parentheses and round brackets and the function they each serve, Sarah Chatel has adopted me as her new friend. [Sarah + Jay (Sarah - Jay) + me] I write on the very back page of my notebook where no one can see. Sarah passes me notes with gold hearts and stars that say, *I can't help it, he's just* so *beautiful. Don't you think he's cute?*

And I draw elaborate seashells and monarch butterflies all over the page, and write back, *Of course I think he's beautiful. Everyone thinks so. You are* so *lucky.*

But, when I hand it back to her, I think *Sarah Chatel you are* so *beautiful. Jay Johnson, you are* such *a poor, helpless, lucky, lucky, lucky, useless prick.*

THE AMATEURS

THE CITY WAS nothing but scaffolding that I could see straight through. My senses had ballooned out of control. I could smell her too. She was bleeding again. I could smell her clear through the fish scent of rain in the markets on garbage day. Her smell preceding her like her red umbrella in the wind. I didn't have to look out my window to know where she was. She was twelve blocks away. All tang and tin. And she was growing closer, stronger.

Scurrying past the travel agent and up the stairs beside Two Nickels Convenience, she held her umbrella out in front of her like a bright pie-shaped shield. The smell of iron and geraniums. Her rubber-soled shoes hitting the grated stairs.

If I turned now I could penetrate all the shops and semihouses between us, watch the door fall shut behind her, and... Onetwothreefour-fivesixseven...see the light come on in the front room of her flat, the red of her coat as she wriggled out of it and hung it over the radiator.

That's how bad it was. I knew exactly where she was. Like an animal scenting out trails. I could smell her, feel her, from this distance, across six streets, though brick and drywall.

I wasn't always this way.

I was supposed to meet my best friend Gavin on Thursday, December 8 at 7:45 p.m. in a coffee shop not far from his studio. Jenny would be there too, briefly, he said apologetically, and that no, he hadn't entered his Carlsberg years and started double-booking his friends. Since she was our age, he assured me that Jenny didn't qualify as his boss, especially since she knew the design work she gave him was a side dish. She was just a freelancer who sometimes hired outside help. He needed some files they had shared. He said it was convenient—she would come, drop off the disks, have a coffee, and then he and I could proceed with our evening plans. Which would, no doubt, include a few high-priced beverages and conversation about exhibitions that hadn't shown yet, and films that he'd seen and that I was still meaning to see.

I arrived first, a little early for once, around 7:35. I went up to the glass counter, took a look at the cheap artificially flavoured coffee selections sludging in burner pots, opted instead for the Tisane—Peppermint.

I sat in the non-smoking section at the second table closest to the door. That way, they would spot me as soon as they arrived. I'd picked up the weekly scene paper. I left it folded in front of me on the table like a prop to justify myself. I stirred my Tisane by way of pulling the string on the bag round and round. I lit a cigarette. Then put it out immediately, realizing I had, after all, picked a table in the non-smoking section. I looked around. No one seemed offended.

A woman with hunched shoulders hurried past the window looking in. Her hair was a white powder puff in the wind, held down by an old-fashioned compact blue hat with a tuft of mesh in the front. A black and blue polka dot scarf sealed her scowl to her body. She looked about eighteen and dressed like she was eighty. Something fierce and fragile. She yanked the door open with a big wintry burst and came in stamping and clapping her fitted leather gloves. She gave the place the once-over, grabbed a black coffee and sat near the back. It wasn't Jenny, who was, by Gavin's detail, "self-conscious and pretty." I was disappointed. My watch said 7:50. This was why lateness was my usual accidental on-purpose; I hated waiting.

A pretty girl with a lazy eye clomped in maybe sixty seconds later. She was tall with Brooke Shields' eyebrows and Julia Roberts' lips. She had on a short jacket and, as if to compensate, tall, clunky shoes. Her black pants bit and nipped in all her narrow parts. I half-stood, but she barely looked at me. She finger-combed her hair for a good three minutes without moving out of the doorway. Then she rather too suddenly recognized the manager and tap-tap-tapped over to the counter to laugh at a head-tipped-back volume with him.

For ten minutes I sat facing the door, tugging my bag around the cup on its string, watching it deposit a leaky tea taste into its pale bath while the little girl was stirring and stirring her medium dark at the back, just behind the busty hyena. Finally, at 8 p.m. on the nose, I decided to approach her—the little girl—maybe just because I wanted her to be Jenny.

There was a severity about her that I liked. Her face was kind of squished into itself, and her eyes and mouth were dark holes in her concentrated head. Squinty and smirky, like black and red jelly beans. Her hat and gloves lay on the chair beside her, and I could see up close that she was naturally white-blonde. No trace of roots. She was sitting in the smoking section and not smoking. She was reading some student-looking volume— a dog-eared classic held open on the sugar-speckled tabletop with one hand, the other hand busy dropping the coffee spoon in and out of her cup between intervals of stirring.

I said her name, the name I hoped was hers. She looked up sharp and quick, as if she hadn't been reading at all.

"Jon," she acknowledged me immediately, and she pushed back the chair opposite her in a most unexpected unladylike manner—with her boot. "Please..." God help me, I know it's ridiculous. Her saying my name and "please," and me sitting down quickly to hide my instant nether reaction. But that's just how it happened. I wouldn't call it love at first sight. More like humiliation at first sight. I was overwhelmed and anxious. She seemed so, too, but it suited her. We made the most menial small talk. She drank her coffee and I drank my tea. When I got up and ordered a beer she said she'd stick to coffee and it was 8:30 and where the hell was Gavin?

I don't think that qualifies as falling in love.

When I came home I could smell the smoke on me from the other smokers, and it wasn't hers, and I'd refrained because she wasn't, and it felt somehow new and sticky and scented as pine incense. I could smell it on my clothes and my hair in a way I never had before. And for weeks when I smoked, when I smelled other people's smoke, I associated that with her.

Finally it was spring. She was sitting on a park bench outside the Art Gallery of Ontario with a camera in her lap. She was eating red licorice, and wearing a red windbreaker and a pair of black clamdiggers.

She saw me first and called my name across the traffic. I was coming home from work at the print shop, walking from University towards Spadina, and the light was 5:30 and perfect, her voice like a strange angel, and she a surprise.

I crossed to her side.

"Take your picture?" she asked, and I played coy. "No, really," she said, and I submitted.

We passed the camera back and forth. She posed in deadpan and also high vogue. She was like a child. I was like a dog chasing my tail, jumping up on the sculptures, poking my face through the crevices and waiting for her clicking tongue.

"Want?" she said, offering up her candy bag. That's how she talked. Without subjects or objects. Everything was abbreviated. As if she had a limited supply to get her through until the next fuel station. She was all verbs.

I said "no," because it seemed too obscene: her 1950s knickers, her sneakers, her vintage Instamatic with the extra-bright flashcube on top, her soda-pop smile and bubble-gum tongue. The way she missed the way I looked at her.

And she said, "In love with my dentist. Been loading my coffee with sugar for months. Eating suckers at all hours. In the hopes that he'll have to bend over me."

"But it's bound to be unrequited, isn't it?" I asked her.

"Mmm." She nodded. "Can't help it. What's there is there. Seem to have this thing for falling for people whose services I pay for. Started with my hairdresser. My vet. Then my dentist. Coincidence?"

Her tone was deadly serious, considering. I shrugged.

She snapped sporadic shots of the sky, the clouds, the way they were settling just then, the light pouring on them like maple syrup. Amateurish and deliberate. I wanted those shots. I wanted them like a proof of her. The set of duplicates. A postcard of a beautiful sunset.

"We must get together," she said with a campy two-handed clutchy handshake, so melodramatic the sentiment seemed genuine.

When I came away, I was carrying a half-bag of her sour-sweet blue raspberry candies in my coat pocket. I would smell her in every artificial tea, every dessert in every restaurant, every fruit drop in every stranger's mouth I passed on the street.

Like I said, I wasn't always this way. I used to date a girl named Danielle. Like all the women I'd admired to that point, she was big, beautiful and rough around the edges, a broad. I adored broads and tomboys. I met her in a bar, and gradually, as the night wore on, they turned the lights dimmer and dimmer. Trying to push the dinner crowd into an evening crowd without anyone noticing. Danielle and I both seemed to notice at about the same time.

"Is it getting dark in here, or what?" she said, tilting her head back.

She was a friend of a friend of a friend. She was a vehement smoker, the way others are political non-smokers. Her cigarettes were exquisite props and she was always pointing them at you while she talked, using them to punctuate each idea she was trying to convey. You got the impression she would put her butts out on your chest if you didn't keep up with her. She said you had no business being in a bar if you weren't going to smoke or drink. We all nodded our heads in agreement because she was loud and confident and had a way of saying things that made them sound like ultimate truth just for a second. We ordered a round and a round and a round and another round.

A few months later I noticed my senses had waned. The same way you don't know your ears are buzzing until you step out of the club. And then you feel the speakers parked inside your head. The streets had gotten darker, more deserted, and I found myself talking much too loudly before I realized it. In the morning my mouth would be full of cement and my nostrils sealed. I didn't smell another thing for the rest of our two-year, live-in relationship.

So Jenny was like a good antihistamine. She was like coming clean sober and getting addicted to all the new smells.

"Who are you in love with now?" I'd ask her when I saw her yellow Oxford shirt bouncing towards me, above her blue wide-leg, pin-striped pants. Her hair cropped short for a new season, a new man who was all woman, like some old Virginia Slims ad. There was a timidness in her she was battling tooth and nail using kilts and stockings and trousers; to me that back-and-forthness made her different than the other parading gallery girls and Queen Street kids.

Her dentist. Her therapist. Her mechanic. She produced crushes from her fist like an endless string of coloured handkerchiefs, solely for my entertainment it seemed. "Still..." she said, shrugging her button chest into breast-sized breasts "...nothing compares to the first. My hairdresser was the best. The touching. The tousling. The tickling duster brush at the end of the cut. Sure he had no clue what it did to me."

Often on that same stretch, halfway between Gavin's studio and mine, Jenny and I collided accidentally on-purpose. We'd grab a coffee or a bite. I found myself going back to specific places I'd run into her, restaurants or little artist-run gallery openings, hoping she might be there again. It was my fault in that respect.

"Who are you in love with now?" I'd ask.

"My mother."

She liked to shake it up sometimes. At least, that's what she said when I pointed out that her mother never got paid to take care of her. Said she had to keep me on my toes.

"Who are you in love with now?"

"You," she said finally. It was June 21 at 10:32 p.m. I had known her—really known her—for over a year.

I think you know right away with someone. Their skin calls to you. That first night. If it doesn't go well, walk away. If it does go well, run like hell. With us, it went both ways.

Jenny's skin was like an open book and I read her like a song I might have memorized years before, forgot, and then found again one day. Found myself prompted by someone else to quote it. Tasted every word on my tongue before I even knew I could sing them.

Our skins rubbed together. Our skins together. Our skins.

We had no bodies. We had no bones. We had only skin. And scent that seeped out from underneath and found its way in.

She like peach candy, sour soothers and Popeye Cigarettes. Me like salt, hickory sticks and Belmont Milds. Soap, sweat, sex.

She rolled on top of me and pulled her knees up, squatting over me, she took me in. She balled her hands into fists in my hands. And I was helpless to her.

But that was all. It was like I couldn't finish because I didn't want it to end. A terrible panic coursed through me and my body bolted like an animal and then jerked back on its leash. And still I couldn't take us as far as I wanted.

When you make a mistake in music class in school as a kid, they tell you not to go back over it or you may make the same mistake twice. But I forgot that advice, and I started at the beginning again.

Our skins rubbing together. Our skins together. Our skins.

And I still couldn't.

So instead, I just pushed the breath out of her. Then she took me in her mouth and slid me into a hard-shelled candy again and again. Why is it that when humans make love it's nothing like the movies? And in spite of that, why was it whenever I went into her, she found a way into me?

"Did you sleep with her?" Gavin wanted to know.

That really irked me. I'd sort of thought he'd be above that type of did-you-or-didn't-you.

But a couple of seconds later, with the look he gave me, I realized he was so casual about it, it was like a guilt-without-guilt kind of question. Almost like he saw my sleeping with Jenny to be a kind of legal heist. The kind of swipe you make when you're actually allowed to take something. Like picking up a book of matches in a restaurant, or keeping the pen with the business's name on it, taking supplies from work. Expected. No biggie.

We were in a restaurant as a matter-of-fact. And he had just been fingering the matches in the clean ashtray. I guess that's what made me think it that way. But in spite of his high school comment, Gavin looked further from high school than any of my other friends. Even though he was my best friend, sometimes he just seemed whiter than the other guys I knew. In his brand name shirts with his cell phone at his elbow on the table, I found it hard to imagine him knowing Jenny outside of me, of having been the one to sort of set us up by accident.

Jenny with her thrift store hats and jackets and her skinny cats, Humphrey and Ingrid, pawing out at us from unexpected hiding places in her pin-box apartment that looked like it had been cleaned each night by fairies—every pen or penny scraped up and placed properly in the orange ashtray or the old-fashioned tobacco tin, the phosphorescent plastic bins, triangular shelves affixed into corners, and CDs arranged into three chrome pillars of equal height: 1) Jazz, 2) Jazz Vocals, Swing and Showtune, 3) Experimental/Indie Rock. Everything was quirky clean, rusted out but gleaming. A modern-day museum where IKEA mated with found objects from Kensington Market or Queen West, and her snapshot-style photography hung overhead blown up to monumental proportions, as if that would make it fine art and grant her access to the world of galleries.

Galleries equalled Gavin's world, come to think of it. The great curator of the show of my life, featuring Jenny. And there he sat with a quiet smirk, fingering the restaurant linens. Portfolio/Day Timer/briefcase guy acting like it was no big deal. I should have known when he put the matches in his pocket and didn't leave quite enough to cover his half of the bill: either he'd already slept with her, or else he wanted to.

"Hate girls like that," Jenny said.

It was a Saturday night out. We had been recounting our childhoods, and on whatever tangent, I'd been describing a friend of my little sister's who'd always gotten second looks from my friends. The kind of girl who was so sweet, she could break their hearts and not even know she'd done it.

"You hate girls like that?" I threw my napkin down in faux disdain. "Guess you're going to have to work on your self-esteem. You can't hate girls like that if you are a girl like that."

She snorted and sucked hard through her straw until the ice rattled.

"Brat," I chided. "Who are you in love with today?"

She looked around the restaurant, as if she was searching for our waiter. He was in the kitchen. "You, I guess."

It was a joke, of course. But the kind that after you hear it more than once, gets stale and you start to wonder what you're doing there eating it.

Gavin got Jenny a show and Jenny gave Gavin more work. Even though he made good money agenting, he still worked a bit doing design for art catalogues, flyers, ads and promo cards. Her main income. He probably didn't need to design; he came from money, and he was organized—the only person I knew from OCAD to ever talk about RRSPs. But he said he couldn't help but dabble in graphic design, that it was his limited way of expressing himself without being a direct competition to his own artists. He seemed to think it was rather big of him.

You may note, I became rather annoyed with Gavin around that time. It might have been a result of Jenny's nonchalant crushes on waiters and record-store clerks, her inability to stay focused on any one thing besides her cats and apartment, or maybe I just saw a different side to Gavin now that I was a couple. And yeah, I was a couple with Jenny. Regardless of her crushes on bookstore clerks, her remote seen-it-before attitude, she was still enthusiastically letting me push the breath out of her.

"Jon," she'd say when we were in bed together, her breasts like flat saucers of milk, "Don't let go of me. Oh...I think I'm about to go...I have to take a little trip now, just hold on to me, so I don't fly off." And then she'd go, and I would watch her face—hers more dear to me than any of the other beautiful contortions women make when they have forgotten to care that you're watching.

Jenny's show was on September 19, at 7 p.m. She was running around getting dressed. Even though she'd bought a houndstooth 40s-style shirt dress, she changed her mind at the last minute and went with basic black. She curled the stray white wisps of her hair into pin curls and put on her pillbox hat.

"You look killer," I told her, pressing my hands into the neat crevices on either side of her backbone.

"Overkill," she argued. She turned around, and since she never wore high heels even though they would have matched her outfits, she stood on tiptoe and kissed me. My eyes were open and the bathroom light streamed around her white hair so I felt like I'd walked into a deep hollow in the heart of a cloud. Meringue.

Did she love me? Did it matter?

I had been granted entrance. That I might not be permitted to stay forever was of no consequence. I had seen this beautiful place and knew it existed. I was there now.

All my life I had felt like Charlie Brown in the Halloween TV special. Like I was going door-to-door, opening up my bag. While the other guys were yelping and hollering over Blow-Pops, Sweet Maries and Snickers, I was peering down through the sloppy eye holes in my ghost sheet, saying, "I got rocks." It's not that I saw her as the Cracker Jack prize, but that I saw her as something different from what I had been given before. And I had been given her, for all my hoping and hunting; she was still very much given.

Gavin couldn't have gotten it more right when he said Jenny was "self-conscious and pretty." I made the mistake of judging her by her habits, the way she dressed. Yet that should have been my first clue. How could I mistake the detail of her day-to-day ministrations for determination? The coordination of skirts and scarves for confidence? How could I miss the way she carried herself...hurried, her words clipped off, the subject omitted.

"Always a wallflower," she said once, of herself in her high school years. When I looked surprised, she amended, "Guess when I turned twenty-one, I decided if you're gonna be a wallflower, might as well be a brightly-coloured one." We both looked down at the yellow hand-knit jumper with the orange-red and brown argyle diamonds across the breasts. A pair of dancer's tights the same blood orange.

Her apartment was obsessive too, in its way. Everything had its place.

Even me. In her bed. Or maybe on the half-size futon couch in front of the 1970s black-and-white TV she insisted suited her needs just fine. And when she made statements like that, it was hard to imagine her as selfish. She was full of such goodness, such a need to give—her constant proferring of iced tea or club soda, kisses or hand jobs—that to get to the centre of that humble soul and find it so full of stoicism seemed obscene.

But there she was, sad and uncertain, and very stoic. She was like a shell. Speckled, delicate. Inside, filled with absence and the roar of the ocean. Like something that was far away from its proper environment.

Seeing Jenny's work hanging in a large white space left a funny feeling in my stomach. The kind of feeling you get after consuming too much fluff at the fair and then riding the Tilt-a-Whirl. It looked very different away from all of her other Jenny things. Sparser, like there was less to it.

The overall sensation was a sense of misplacement. I had the inkling that there might have been something spectacular in the very next frame, but she had chosen the wrong shot, always hovering at the edges of what she really wanted to express. Everyone was working with the fleetingness of joy just then; all the films and books that had been coming out were using non-linear structures and forgoing plots to explore simply the notion of memory. The cloud shots were there, enclosed in chrome frames, hanging cleverly from the twenty-foot ceiling. A flattened black-and-white representation of the real thing. I knew that Gavin's gallery counterpart, Naz, hadn't been pleased. It had taken the three of them ten hours of attempts to install those prints alone.

I want to say that I was impressed, if not because of the work then because of affection, but I wasn't. Art is the one thing we must never lie to ourselves about. Jenny's portraits were vaguely Ansel Adams meets Nan Goldin and the family album. Overly stark, black-and-white nature shots interspersed with close-ups of people bouncing out of frame. I wasn't embarrassed for her, it was up-to-par; it just wasn't terribly original.

On the ride over as she'd nosed her corroded Parisienne through the traffic she'd confided that there was a picture of me in the show. She grabbed my hand at the stoplight and looked at me with guilty pleasure, like she had just spilled the beans on a Christmas or birthday gift. It was extremely endearing and I kissed her fingers before she had to snatch them back to grip the wheel. I felt my heart lurch forward with the huge vehicle.

Seeing myself on a wall was less flattering. I was too self-conscious to stand in front of it and stare at myself. Instead, I spared quick glances from across the room, where I stood between Jenny and Gavin who were often otherwise engaged. Jenny, almost solemn with the occasion, spoke softly, unsmilingly to casual friends some of whom warranted introductions and others who didn't; Gavin was engaged with what he was good at—selling.

Was this how Jenny saw me? I was tucked into the top right corner of the frame, cut off at the forehead. My head tipped, I was making big dark puppy eyes, my hands bent at my chest like shadow puppets. In the background the obsidian edges and orifices of the statue in front of the AGO. I know what she was trying to show, this juxtaposition of amorphous and volcanic: what was cerulean blue now erupted in pale bubblish grey light beyond the holes in the black stone, and the expression on my face was one of pure tenderness and wanting. I realized she must have known from the first time I met her how I felt. Now that feeling was on display. I looked like an idiot.

"Why that one?" I whispered in her ear, perplexed and embarrassed.

"Don't like it?" She was hurt. We both turned and stared at it.

"I look like a dork," I said.

"I love the way you look there." Her voice was wistful as she looked back at me. It was the first time she had parked the "I" next to the "love." "You're so unleashed in that picture. *My* Jon."

We both looked again.

The rectangular foamcore card tucked to the wall held the title in its small white lap: *Rendezvous #2*.

"Maybe it's because of that day," she admitted, looking at the work with a cooler eye, more detachment. "That was a great day," she said, shaking her head, the same way one might say, "That was a great movie" or "That was a great album" about something you hadn't seen or heard in a long time.

"Yeah," I said quietly, "it was."

It never occurred to me to ask about her and Gavin. But gradually, the clues became obvious.

He had become much freer with his money. That was the first thing. When we went out on Fridays, he began to make a big production of paying for both of us, and his tips increased too, come to think of it. Then again, he also had new toys. A brand new laptop, new shoes, new cell, new pieces for his home collection. At first I was worried that he was dipping into his artists' money. There were rumours that they weren't getting paid on time. He started writing off our meals and drinks together as business, which everyone does, but managing one-step-beyond-art-school artists wasn't exactly big business... Something wasn't right. It was something besides bad bookkeeping. It was guilt spending.

"I'm worried about Gavin," I said to Jenny one night.

"Oh," she said. I found that kind of weird. She never just said "oh." I thought she would rattle off some subjectless information, what was happening with her show, with the other shows, with the design she was getting him to do, something about stress and all that. Or that she would ask why, why was I worried? But in retrospect, I guess she didn't have to ask why because she knew. In that respect, she never lied.

"Who are you in love with?" I asked her, stepping up behind her where she was washing dishes in her sink. Her skin, a sweet tart of sweat where the hair had been shorn up her neck, honey and lemon. I felt curls of hair at her ear beneath my lips like the white suds breaking between her fingers.

She stiffened, and didn't say anything for a breath too long. "You," she said, then, "and Gavin."

Every guy can sniff out another. You can meet someone once and know where they've been. Judge a man as simply as shaking his hand. Is he good enough to date your sister? Is he good enough to be your friend? The problem is that these two answers are not always the same.

It was all fine and good for me to drink micro-brew beer with Gavin on Thursday or Friday evenings. To discuss DJs and magazines and independent films. To watch women in polyester leopard print come and go while talking of D'Angelo. To tie on a few too many sometimes and get downright crass on occasion. Still, there were lines that weren't crossed. I understood Gavin's loneliness and his annoying need to impress, to try to pass for something more than he was, to be one of the beautiful people. He understood my choice to subvert my own talent by working as a lackey at a living wage, making half-tones of other peoples' large conceptions. My understated wardrobe of plaid shirts, navy workshirts or sweater vests, my desire to express life in its basest and simplest terms—cyan magenta yellow black—to eat, drink, sleep, love and perhaps one day reproduce. These things were, they were not said. And because they were not said, Gavin could not say the other things.

That he hadn't shown up that first night I met Jenny, because he didn't think he was worthy of her wanting. And then that he still wanted her anyway, in spite of the detour he had arranged for her. From what little I had to work with, that was the best I could figure. They had been involved before, sort of, but not.

He was right. He wasn't worthy. He was too trendy to put on old sweaters or old CDs. I played "Little Wing" just for her. He was too driven to be happy just watching black-and-white TV for hours as a means of holding her hand. He was too pompous to see without being seen, to give without taking. In short, he was the kind of guy I would never leave alone with my sister.

I should have been furious. At other points in history, men would fight and kill to keep their women. Instead, I was completely calm. It's not like I was living in an unsettled land or a time of war or poverty. My problem was small in comparison to the scope of human suffering. So be it. My best friend and my girlfriend. Who was I to intervene? I stepped back and watched the water drain.

Those next few weeks were full of falling. Everywhere in my apartment she had touched, I felt her presence. I knew her schedule and I could imagine exactly what she would be doing at any given moment that I might forget to not think. There was a rational amount of rage, but it settled over me like dust. And outside, the rain fell. I could smell her even in the rain, from across the city. Could picture her smile. Trace her steps. Her small hand in Gavin's. Or wrapped around the curved handle of her umbrella. Her fingers splayed. Her sad-happy eyes squinting through the weather. Her mouth that had kissed me. That had said, "Hold on." That had said my name. That had said, "You."

Where she really was, I must not have ever known. All I knew was her skin, and the things it told me without telling me. It told of love and transcendence. Meanwhile, clothed, she told me of her hairdresser, her veterinarian, her dentist. The whole time she had told me there was someone else, she just couldn't say that it wasn't any of those people.

Jenny went away without giving either of us any notice. I had stopped calling her apartment anyway, and then one day, Gavin phoned and said that he'd heard through some other artists that Jenny had given away the cats and left Toronto. She'd moved to New York.

"Do you think she'll make it?" I asked. It was the first conversation he and I had had since everything fell apart.

"Not in art," he said with vehemence and I wondered what, if anything, had occurred between them. "But otherwise," he said softly, more softly than I could remember ever hearing Gavin speak, "yes, I think she will, in some way."

So little time had passed in comparison to the time in my mind. It was a Saturday in November. Saturday, November 21, 11:15 a.m. The kind of last perfect day in the world. A cold day where the streets seem polished by the wind, but everyone is out in long coats with their dogs and kids because of the sunshine, as hazy as smoke, settling between the buildings, pooling low and heavy in the belly of the city. Torn yellow leaves thrown up, billowing against glass. Damp gutters from the weeks before. She was gone.

My heart sang and my body mourned. In tandem the two moved around the apartment, picking things up and putting them down again.

In a strange way, it was as if being with Danielle had prepared me to be with Jenny, so didn't it follow that having been with Jenny would also lead me on to something else? It was only that I didn't know what yet.

It was a good day to move forward. A good day to buy art supplies. What had I been waiting for? I was barely thirty-two years old, and no worse than anyone else out there. I would begin working at it immediately, I promised myself as I rode the streetcar across Queen.

People got on and off at every stop. I noticed how the light licked the neck hairs of the woman sitting in front of me, small golden shoots concentrated in the centre and fanned off behind her ears like the V of a bird faraway in flight. An old woman in a checked coat got on with a shopping bag and someone in the front gave up their seat. Lovely, I thought, staring out the window again. The world could still be lovely.

When I'd gotten my things, I decided not to start right away, but to let the ideas creep into me. I went to the Bata Shoe Museum that afternoon. Maybe to see the place where fashion and art meet. I didn't come up with any answers or ideas there. I sat outside afterwards and sheltered a cigarette from the wind. It was 5:30 and the clouds were setting in a swollen cobalt sky. I looked through the buildings and thought about the places outside of the city where farmers would be raking up the leaves and burning them, setting fires along the ditches and watching the black smoke rising up, the definitive smell of autumn that I remember only from childlike moments of driving past.

ACCESSORIES

I LOOKED REALLY good that year. I had a Farah Fawcett haircut and a pair of bitch-red boots way before anyone else. I had a sparkling cherry clasp on my white leather belt. I was so rocker chick before it happened. I had just come out of my Hello Kitty phase and I was like the nemesis to myself. How to get from Barbie pink to hardcore in six weeks without rebuilding your CD tower. My God, I could've written the column. It was like all these guys would just come up to me. It didn't matter where I was. I just looked that good. And I felt like I was always saying something unexpected, even to myself. Really witty, you know. Like one minute I'd be all chill, the silent ice princess and the next I'd be all animated, scotch on the rocks and "Here's looking at you, kid." I was a broad, a real broad, you know what I'm saying?

Just that year. It was so good like that. I just felt...I don't know...like I was making things happen. I had music in me. I felt in control.

Oh, look at this. This guy. I slept with him. Oh. My. God. I can't believe I'm telling this story. He was like...I met him at this party that I wasn't even supposed to be at. One night, I was out with Jan and Angel, and we were downtown. We were dressed, you know. I mean I was still all rocker, like I'm saying, but it was a little more subdued that night. What was I wearing? Oh, I don't remember, but we were passable for chic anyway. We had trouble getting parking so we were on this residential street, you know, townhouses, studio buildings. And there's this condo party going on right there on the first floor, sliding doors, a few really swank-looking guys smoking outside because, right, what kind of loser would smoke inside at someone's condo-warming? So we parked the car, and they looked at us, and we looked at them. And me and Angel and Jan just knew. We didn't say a word to each other. We all just turned and headed up the walk, like that's why we'd been on that street in the first place.

And the guy, Claude, yeah like "cloud." He said, you must be Talia, Hilary said you'd be bringing some friends. So, since he was talking to me, I wasn't about to go, no, my name's Carrie and like I don't even know anyone here I just thought I'd walk up your pseudo-homeowner's postage-stamp lawn and hang out on one of your back-breaking wrought iron patio chairs, you know, enjoy your cityscape and drink your hundred-dollar wine. So I'm like, yeah, this is Vanessa and Brie, 'cause like I'm gonna call them Jan and Angel at a party like that. Me, suddenly I'm Talia. I don't even know how to pronounce it really, what ethnicity is it, do you know? And who's Hilary I'm thinking, because this guy is just too good to be true. Well, I mean look at him.

I always liked hitting on guys I wasn't supposed to, you know, even back in the day. I'd be riding the metro in my jeans and Ts, looking like the stereotypical student and some forty-year-old business slickster would be sitting next to me, pressed pants and perfume. God I love clean-shaven men, especially when they're right fresh and you can smell the lotion on them. Oh...but anyway...

So yes, this is his condo and Hilary's inside, his wife I was guessing though he wasn't wearing a ring. And I'm obviously supposed to know Hilary, so I say, well I'll just pop in for a second and say hello. So I go in and check out the pad, stop off in the bathroom to kill a bit more time. When I come back out, he's like, didn't she give you a glass of wine? And I'm like, oh she was talking to someone and I didn't want to interrupt, I'll just catch up with her in a bit. So he sends one of the other guys in with Angel to get us some drinks and we get cozy real fast. Now I mean, I have a conscience. Don't look at me like that, I do. But it was just such a riot and I was really just playing along to see how far I could take it before we got thrown out. I never really expected it to go so far.

Don't get the wrong impression, nothing happened that night. Claude was just like, I *have* to see you again. We *must* talk. So I gave him my cell number, not like I expected him to call. And I was like, yes in my work it's just so seldom I meet anyone so *fresh*, so open. Two hours we'd been talking and I don't even know what line of work Talia was supposed to be in. "Fresh," I remember I used that word a lot though. It just seemed like a movie script word and I wanted to say it when I was there because the whole thing was such a private drama. He worked from home, so I wound up going there to see his stuff. Sort of a come-up-and-see-my-etchings thing, and oh by the way would you like to touch my chisel? Seriously, he was a sculptor. Shit yes. I mean, I thought all sculptor's were gay but look at that body. Geez I think she must have supported him. I did-n't even think about it at the time, I just thought, you know, rich people are rich. She was in film, I don't know exactly what she did but she must have been pretty up there 'cause their place was like a leather furniture store and Claude picked me up a couple times in a—Oh yeah, it went on for a while, we were snogging all the time.

Well, just a couple times actually.

I felt really bad, you know, I just couldn't do it. He talked about her all the time. After a while I felt like I knew more about Hilary than I did about him. I mean the sex was really great but it was really terrible too. I just couldn't do it. That's probably the worst thing I've ever done in my life. He gave me some jewellery, and it was really sweet, you know, these teardrop earrings. I never have anyplace to wear them though, they're not really me. But he was like, I know we can't keep doing this but I just wanted to give you something beautiful, because I'll never forget you and I don't want you to forget either. He was so good that way. You know, I mean he could've just said, look my wife's going to find out if we keep doing this, so here's some-thing to keep quiet. I mean, I'm not naive, I understand how a gesture like that could appear. But it really didn't have that connotation at all. He made everything so romantic, you know.

No, of course I told him my real name. I mean, what kind of girl screws some guy under an assumed name? Right, I mean, that's like some trick guys in bars use. Come on.

Although, the first time we did it, he still thought my name was Talia. I hadn't figured out a way to tell him at that point, so he didn't know until the second time. So the first time, he's all like, *Tal-ia Tal-ia Tal-ia*, while we're doing it. I know, it was so bad. I really did feel like I was in a movie, playing a part. It was kind of nice, you know, hearing him say this name over and over again, so imbued with emotion, almost like because it wasn't mine I could believe in the fantasy, believe he really meant it.

But you know, that's actually how I met Vincent. You met Vincent that once, remember, we ran into you at the Film Festival? Well, basically, what happened was Claude called me up about four months after our...tryst, asked if I might be interested in going to a premiere as a date for a friend of his. Well, I told you before how that went. That pretty much ended my rocker chick phase. I got all taupe, I wore nothing but white and beige and grey.

You never saw our place, did you? Well, I mean I was only there for the summer. Yeah, last May through September. This is us at the dining-room table. We used to get up and shower together every single morning before having breakfast. Yeah, yeah he was nearly bald on top, but don't you think he's still sexy in that older-man way? This is us at his piano. He was really unbelievable. He kept saying that maybe he could give me lessons, but I mean, well we just didn't get around to it. I thought we'd have all this time. Oh, but can you see this painting in the background? I bought that for him myself. I did. Me, I was an art buyer for one day of my life! I got to walk into this gallery and be the hotshot. I knew he wanted it, so I saved up all my paycheques, put on Claude's teardrop earrings, walked in in this open-backed white pantsuit and was like, I'd like this delivered to Mr. Valente...You know, I thought he would see the goodness in me through the gesture, but to him it was just money. Something new and interesting to show his friends. To me, that's my time and my income, four months worth, hanging on his wall. Guess I can't ask for it back, eh?

Well, whatever.

This is us in the kitchen. It had been just such a perfect day. We had gone shopping for these really cool goblets. God. In retrospect it was so boring. I mean, we had all these nice things and we just sat on the balcony all the time drinking wine and ordering the kind of take-out that I didn't know you could get delivered to your home. But it was like, well, after the summer was over, it's like what else is there? There's not much else to do but have kids, you know, become the little wife until he gets restless and needs a mistress named Carrie that gets called Talia. You know, I don't think it's that fun to be either the wife or mistress. I guess if there's one thing I learned from living with Vincent, that'd be it.

I really did love him though, you know. I loved the way he looked from the back when he was getting dressed in the morning. I loved the mole on his neck and the hair on his forearms. Sometimes I would just sit and look at him. Just sit and look. Just...I don't know why it didn't work out. He just...He just didn't want me. I was like a novelty or something. He was too old for me really, in retrospect.

You know, I really just want an Asian boyfriend now. Maybe I'll get a tattoo on my shoulder, like the symbol for Peace or Friendship or something. Something really, from within, you know, that I can wear on the outside. I mean, I just think Asian men are really where it's at. I know, this is like a stereotype but I think it's a positive one, so that makes it all right, doesn't it? They're just so hardworking and good-looking, everything in one package, you know. They're lean and they stay so young-looking. And they have real values not like these rich clowns I was into the past couple years. I mean, while we're talking about stereotypes, a couple years ago the thing was to have an Asian girlfriend, absolutely all the guys I knew were into that. But to have an Asian boyfriend, that's...you know, it's like twisting the tables.

Oh, yeah, that's a picture of Lydia. She was my best friend. I mean, really, she was the best friend I ever really had. That's a really sad story. That picture was taken like ten years ago, but it could've been taken last week. She's just never really progressed, you know. She's still into that whole hippie thing. She looks exactly the same as she did when she was twenty-two.

We just, we don't really have anything in common anymore. Well, we were always like yin and yang. But it's like she's such a shut-in now. She only goes to coffee shops, never bars, or else she sits in her apartment, reading. Just reading. Like she can't get away from this idea of what it is she's sup-posed to be. I think she has this notion that she's still going to save the world, but really she's just like anybody else. You know, she's got her peti-tions and her activist study groups and her job for one human rights org or another, but you know, she's just jumping from one issue to another all the time. I think she just can't stand to look at herself so she has to focus on everyone else's problems. Well, who could stand to look at that? She just never really takes care of herself, you know. You know, you have to.

But I mean, because I gave all that up, I think Lydia thinks I've lost my ideals. I still have ideals, I'm just focusing on me right now. I'm really working on myself. Meanwhile, it's like she's still pushing papers for the man, it's just a different man. You know, one with a goatee or something like that.

Yeah, that's what I'm saying. We used to do all that stuff together, all these fundraisers and protests, it was so exciting. It was like a big party except you were there with like a purpose. I felt so united with all these really interesting people. But I don't know, after a while it just seemed so pointless. They were always looking down on me 'cause the food I brought to the potlucks wasn't organic. And it was like one week you weren't supposed to buy grapes and the next week you weren't supposed to buy bananas because of the treatment of workers in third world countries, but you couldn't even call them Third World because that was so un-PC. It's funny though, they never ever said not to buy coffee, probably because they were all fucking addicts. It's like I tried so hard, but I could never keep track of all the Dos and Don'ts, like there should've been a column or something. I felt like I just didn't know enough to really make a difference.

The only cause I could ever really get behind was the plight of the homeless really. 'Cause if you don't have family, you can lose everything so fast. Just like that. That's why I'm really lucky to have so many good friends. You know, I've always been grateful that it's easy for me to meet people and just be myself, you know. There are so many people, just good people who do things for me. I mean, it's like even Claude was looking out for me, setting me up with Vincent like that.

Yeah, me and Lydia were really close though. She was like my sister. When she was in my life, I just knew that I would always be okay. I still call her sometimes, but I feel like she always has something else she has to do. She always seems to have to get off the phone in a hurry. She's really... Yeah, she's just...so sad.

WATERING THE DARK

1

Everywhere I looked people were crying. Something terrible had happened. Old men on park benches wept from their translucent, watery old-
men eyes. Young women, outside of churches and schools, bent to adjust
the cuffs on their jeans or the lines of their slips, only as a device to bend,
to hide their flushed weepy faces as I passed to save us both the embar-
rassment. Some people cried with their eyes; others with their motion. But
even the people who weren't crying still seemed...affected. That year.
Something terrible—I didn't know what.

2

The tiny man huddled against the subway wall letting chords ricochet at
odd angles up the stairs, his metal voice crying out of tight plastic lungs, his
thin frame sagging against the concrete blocks as if this pumping, sighing
old instrument strapped across his chest could illicit security, currency.
Between trickling fingers: another country, another time, another man
played it more jubilantly, a polka for a polka-dot-skirted girl in high-heeled
shoes. Every day the wheezing rush of running shoes tripped an eyeful of
empathy, a handful of nickels and dimes.

3

But worse were the women, staring at nothing. All of them in lines outside the malls or the markets in the morning: black stockings with flat black shoes. Blouses—white, black or dark blue. Watching the sky for an open door.

4

And one woman my age, outside the laundromat, was gasping for air at the end of a cigarette, picking the dog hair off her black tights, square-carved teeth behind blood-streak lipstick, fingernails, tight hair, loose sweater misshapen wool miswashed many times and stretched and restretched. Cigarette smoke fell out of her upper lip, falling out solid as an object—or something with impact—a hiccup. A sob. Sadness, a cup of water. The cigarette white as soap.

5

Everyone was sad.

6

That year my best friend, Dan, began to write a poem. He called it "There Is No One Who Will Take Care Of You." So far as I know it was the instrumental equivalent of a poem; it had no words. Only its title which Dan repeated again and again—to me in bars, to his classmates at the university, to his lover over the phone. Something so abstract and obvious.

"There Is No One..."

"There Is No One..."

Its notes, a resilient chorus in my head even after all this time. Its chorus, its cadence, its chaos.

6

They were publishing great novels about great turmoil in quiet corners; perhaps that was what this was all about. A marching band of misanthropes was what I wanted. Not this bullshit stuff on paper—words likes squeamish notes dripping from one to the next without saying anything. Under Dan's adamant supervision I read all the books I was supposed to, but none of them said anything to me. The brave ones cried. The scared ones sulked. Something in between was missing.

4

Every week, the laundromat girl had collected more dog hair. Her tights grew tighter. Her lipstick redder. Her ponytail rigid as wax. Her mouth crackling, spitting smoke out at the sidewalk in front of her. Her clothes reeking of wet dog, and detergent, and plaster.

6

Aspiring writers had stopped writing about the world and started writing about themselves. That's what was wrong.

"You're what's wrong," Dan told me, poking a fuzzy digit in my distracted direction.

5

The whole world was blurry. Lights bleared into night and I lost my cool in the toilet. Everything came tumbling out. And in the morning light would bleed into my room like milk. I would wake bleary and wash. And wash. And wash. I was not so much a wreck as I make it sound. I functioned rather normally in fact. As is usual to people who are extremely self-conscious. People who are apologetically sad.

3

The old women outside of the discount stores began eyeing me suspiciously. It was as if they knew. When I walked past, a gutterful of rain fell out of me, gathering up the bubble-gum wrappers and old scraps of newpaper in its surge. They stopped looking at the sky and started looking at their feet. They covered their heads with their black shawls. Some fumbled in their handbags, unbuckling the terrible clunky clasps with the click and cluck of unforgivable pity, impulsive acts of fear and charity. They waved 2-for-1 coupon clippings, church circulars, bandages, dollar bills. They shouted at me in Portuguese, Italian, Polish or German depending on the street. I had affected them without intending to. These were their offerings, their sympathies.

5

I was a deity of misery.

6

Dan and his cronies collected in empty pubs. They wore sweater vests and corduroys and believed that they were reinventing a fashion trend with an added twist of irony. I wore tight black shirts with jeans and believed myself, somehow, less obvious. My chair pulled up quietly in the shadow of their gaiety.

"We haven't found the chord," they said of contemporary poetry.

And... "We are still listening to eulogies. We have only eulogies and pop songs, there is no poetic democracy."

I jumped up and put the market women's quarters in the juke box, punched in jazz and blues selections in some desperate search for the America in it all. As if to prove them wrong. Always the tagalong tagging on some kind of silent last line.

They laughed and their laughs tremored with an obvious nervousness, as if I had interrupted a necessary discussion that would now find no resolution. As if something could have been done about our entire literary history— future—if only their heads weren't swimming in erratic trumpet solos and imagined smoke—their mouths taut o's with chuckles and hoots, not so distantly related to wailing.

5

The afternoon evaporated into evening like week-old dishwater, slowly, streaking the chrome with a ring of pale residue. The night poured into the cup in my hand like black coffee. When I looked up to see who had poured it, no one was there.

5

I stumbled past boarded-up storefronts and burned-out music halls, laundromats and watering holes with neon signs halflit—burned-out halfwords, letters forming new slogans I wanted to find amusing but found only disconcerting.

6

"There Is No One..."
"There Is No One Who Will..."
"There Is No One..."

2

"Hey Kid."
The voice hovered, disconnected from its source.
"Kid."

Again, like a tossed object, the sound of it pinging like a penny on the sidewalk at my feet. A short man was slumped on the park bench, doubled into the wooden boards, torn to the elbows, shoes without laces. I had no more quarters—I patted coat pockets for cigarettes.

"Spare a few words of wisdom?" he leered, as hideous as if he had just suggested sodomy with a screwdriver.

5

I ran. My boots banging asphalt like little hammers of rain. And it started to rain. I ran until I came to a place I knew.

4

The laundromat was lit like a stage and it was only from that distance that I saw for the first time, with perfect clarity, its symmetry: its long lines of white washers, its empty tubs on the end, its yellow folding table through the centre, its single orange chair with the cracked plastic back facing the street.

She was there, almost as if she had never left. She had stopped pulling dog hair from her clothes altogether. She was carpeted in new layers. Her ponytail was unfathomably long, split ends tickling the top of her tight tights. She butted out her cigarette and looked at me like she'd been expecting me. Her lips were strangely pale with the light behind her.

"Where have you been?" she said, her voice as thin and glassy as her lit hollow backdrop. "You look like hell."

5

I dropped into the orange plastic chair and there she nursed me on salt and vinegar potato chips and Coke from the machines in the corner. My tears were drying into the salt crumbs of chips fallen on my chest, drying into the broken raindrops beaded on my arm hair, drying into the static and softener in the dryers' thundered mumbling to the muddy stains that were setting inside their huge tumbling drums.

Drying.

7

When the drying was done, she asked me to carry the basket. We walked through an alley and up a steep flight of iron stairs to a dark narrow apartment, like I knew we would. I stood in the doorway, appointing myself the position of silhouette for lack of anything else to be in that scene. She took off her bumpy black sweater and underneath it was the whitest undershirt I had ever seen.

The dog came over to nose my knees, and that was when I knew I had known this dog and this girl before, very well, that perhaps I had even lived there and the dog had slept on my feet to keep me grounded. All I could remember was rainy grey, and a line of a poem I must have read somewhere, and the faces of strangers, but the dog seemed to be able to read every colour of every coat I had passed, the content of every crack I had stepped on or over. It listened to the history on me with its snout. The dog kept sniffing and sniffing, and I knew I must have been gone a very long time.

SUBSTITUTE

THERE IS THE world around me, and then, there is the world inside my head. I know of all the struggles in this life—the only one that really matters is the struggle between these two. Days like today though, I just want to blame it on my twin sister.

Right now Tina is the red-faced one on the field. I'm the white-faced one on the sidelines. Watching the game while picking the scab on my knee, pretending like it doesn't matter. That she's out there and I'm not. That we're down 2-nothing. About halfway through the second half. We could still come back. Tina's shouting "Move up!" to the defensive line, because she wants to play it tight, get the calls on the offsides. She's number 12, the sweeper.

I used to play defence, but now I play right wing forward. Defence was just a muddle when there were two of us back there. After three years, our goalie still has rocks for brains and can't tell us apart.

"Dina's ball!" I'd yell, claiming it, two steps away.

Crystal, the keeper, would be on it anyway, practically colliding with me. "Oh," she'd say, giving it a drop kick or, if she was out of her box, hammering it fast out of bounds, "Sorry, I thought you were calling your sister to take it but I was closer."

"Dina," I'd say as I walked away from her, "D—Dina."

"Yeah, yeah. Sorry."

There are a few things bothering me about this game. First off, I'm the one who shows up at practice. Tina's been too busy blowing this guy, Brad Bellows, to come out on Wednesday nights to do head balls and corner kicks. So figure that out. After a good first half on my part, coming back to help out defence, what am I doing still sitting on the sidelines, twenty-five minutes through the second half? Ms. K. is usually pretty fair about these things. Am I not wearing a number on my back? Tina's shirt did not get mixed up with mine in the laundry. I'm 24. Tina's 12. 12, 24, these are like, opposite numbers right? No mistaking them.

Okay, okay, let it go, Dina, I have to tell myself.

My mother's here. That's the second thing. Why is my mother here? I can see her from here, on the back row of the bleachers directly across the field from where I'm sitting. She is drinking out of a hard plastic slushie cup with a rigid straw, the cooler beside her, probably full of pops for us after the game, which you may think is sweet, except that it may not be, and we didn't tell her we were playing a home game tonight. If I'm perfectly honest with myself, and with you, it wasn't a mistake. We don't want her here tonight. Either of us.

"That's right, Tina." She's on her feet, clapping. "Move it up, move it up. Let's get this game back, girls!" It's cold for June, and her red-and-white windbreaker billows out from her stick body like a Canadian flag. The last time I asked my mother when we were having dinner, she told me she got a special on chicken pot pies, three for a dollar, and I could throw one in the oven if I was so hungry. I was twelve then. Since then it's been pot pie for me and liquid dinner for them. My mother drinks wine or beer, occasionally Canadian Club whiskey. Tina drinks Coke or coffee or Slimfast or some other power shake. (I guess that's the reason she's sucking face and I'm only dancing with pylons.)

After supper, I usually just fall asleep on my bed until the evening hours have dribbled away. My mother passes out around eight-thirty, Tina takes off for Brad's, and I have the house to myself. Though, sometimes, it's easier to sleep through than to fill up that space that isn't quite empty. My mother's hollow face, brown glass arms and legs sticking out from the couch, her head tipped back, open at the mouth, her clothes stickered to her wherever she has spilled, sweated or leaked. Only her belly protrudes from the couch. The rest of her has shrunk. Her midsection is small but swollen as a kid's T-shirt stuffed with the pregnancy of a basketball—or something slighter—one of those red rubber dodge balls from grade school. I move around the snoring softly, as if my footsteps might kick something over inside both of us, and wake us up.

Right now, the play has flown into the far end of the field and Janine and Joy are passing the ball back and forth around one lone defenceman. Janine and Joy are the only other sister combo on the team, the Jacobses, with Janine two years older, better, and bossier. They play centre forward and centre halfback. "Come on," I coax them, under my breath. "Come on, just one." If they can figure out who's going to take the shot, we'll have it. It's Joy, in spite of the fact that Janine is calling her for another pass.

I could have told her that on a give-and-go, you hardly ever get back what you give. Everyone wants something for themselves, even when they know it's not for the good of the team.

The goalie's been drawn out too far, forced to play it aggressive because her lazy-ass defence line are *walking* back from half. As if they didn't think we could hit the target. Joy fakes the pass, throwing her body like she's going to send it sideways, then bang, straight into the bottom left corner.

"It's just one, it's just one," their team's yelling to themselves, as everyone on our side jumps up, whooping, high-fiving, running up to the half mark to clasp hands or slap Joy and Janine on the back.

Ms. K. looks at me. "It's been in our end the whole game. Your sister's been holding the fort, but she looks like she's going to pass out. You mind going back on D.?" Before I can answer, "Substitution," she yells to the ref, one arm raised so he can't miss it.

I stop picking my scab and pull my socks up. "Nicki hasn't been in all this half," I say quietly, so Nicki won't hear me. She's standing up, about ten feet behind us. Probably the only person on the team who's shyer than me. See what I mean about that whole exterior vs. interior

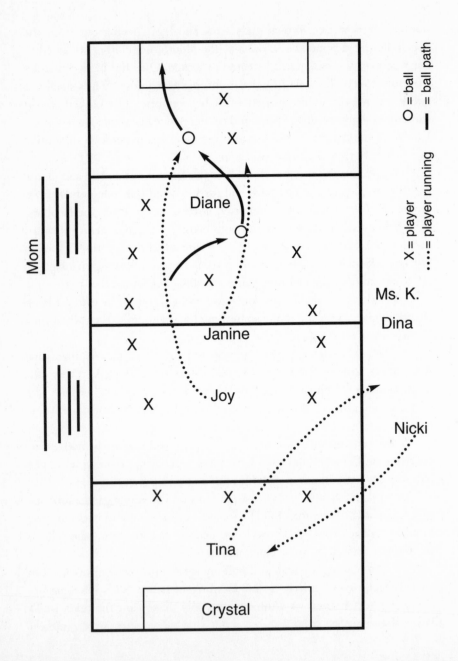

thing? I bet you thought I was a real b with an itch, didn't you? The way this sideline soliloquy's been going...

"Tina!" Ms. K. calls her off. Twice of course, because Tina doesn't want to hear her. Ms. K. shoots me a quick quiet look that I can't interpret. My dad used to give me that look sometimes. Just before he left two years ago, Tina would refer to it as the *honourable martyr presiding* look. I'm not sure if she meant me or him. "Nicki, take Tina off," Ms. K. says over her shoulder.

"Janine..." Ms. K. calls. Oh boy, is Janine gonna be pissed. Her sister gets the shot and Ms. K. doesn't give her a chance to get back into the action. "Get your butt up to centre, Dina. I expect a shot within the first two minutes."

So much for toeing the chalk outlines around my life. I'm up and running.

Tina crosses over the sideline as I'm heading out. She grabs the water bottle off the grass, guzzling it back until it runs down her chin and under her shirt. Her eyes are pure turquoise peeling out of apple-red skin. "You can do it! Bring us up to score," she calls between mouthfuls when she sees me glancing back.

That's another problem. On both sides. It's hard to hate someone who has the same face as you.

"Dina, watch Number 36," Janine tells me as she passes. "Gave me a freakin' elbow to the tit after the shot. That's why Ms. K. pulled me. Holy...I was gonna deck 'er."

Janine's talking about Diane Wells. One of my best friends in grade nine and ten before she transferred. I still played defence, so we played together then. Before Ms. K. was our coach. Diane was fast, smooth, confident and loud. The kind of girl who drew the grade-twelve guys into the bleachers even though they couldn't possibly have cared about junior girls' soccer. Maybe that's why Diane and I hit it off. She was slick and lively; I was attracted to that and she probably saw me as the ideal silent sidekick: someone with enough brains, brawn and beauty to keep up, but not enough raw drive to overshadow her—her or anybody. She was a dirty player, but she was on my side then.

Once I saw her wrap her hands around a girl's throat when they tangled ankles and went down. I think she honestly might not have let go if I hadn't yelled her name loud enough to make the ref stop the play that had continued. After that she never really forgave me for playing so clean. She said it must be part of some kind of virgin complex. At parties she would single me out and slag my clothes or hair, or the way I talked. Try to get me drunk. Only in the name of friendship, of course. She didn't want me to get left out, she said.

Now she's standing there on the eighteenth yard line, hands on hips, looking like she can't believe they'd bother putting me on centre forward.

The other team's taken as long with their subs as we have and the ref looks a bit pissed. He blows the whistle for the kickoff before their right winger is really in position and she misses the pass. Joy's on it right away and sails the ball up the field. It's either mine or Diane's now. She's got it but it's bouncing high, out of control, and I'm nearly on top of her for it.

"Fuck off, Daniels," she says, bringing her elbows up the second I get my foot on the ball. It richochets between our bodies, hitting her groin and my knees, knocked from one set of shin guards into the other. We're both drilling at it, but it's deadlocked between us, held in place between our ankles. I smell breath and sweat as dense as if my face were pressed into her crotch, and know she can smell the same sour scent from me. That and the chemical talcum taints of her cover-up and hairspray trickling off. I back off a half a step. She's still trying to get it loose. Taps the ball right to me.

I knock it into the empty space to the right of me, about ten feet, and I'm about to lunge after it, when I hear the scuffle of cleats and the call, "Joy's ball."

So now I'm passing Diane on the left and Joy's dribbling up the centre. Diane's all over her, and there's one indecisive defenceman on the right, far enough back that there's no fear of offsides if Joy tabs it through. "Here, Joy..."

It's a perfect pass. Halfway between me and the goalie, drawing her out. She's already crouching but it's still three feet away from her, and I don't slow down. I let my weight shift forward to my toes, propelling me on, light-footed, so I don't cripple her if I make contact. I get a toe on it just as it hits the tips of one glove. My first instinct is to smash it towards the net, but my weight is off for using my right foot. I find myself just running straight through. Jumping over her and toeing it all the way into the goal.

I'm more aware of the goalie swearing than of our team cheering. Then Joy grabs me around the waist and swings me around, whooping. I can't help but laugh. We start jogging back down the field to our end.

"Substitution!"

Janine's back on the field to my right. She pulls Cecilia, and tells Joy to switch positions with Katja, so the Jacobs sisters are flanking me. I'm surprised that Janine's back in already, but the game has gone from a win to a tie in three and a half minutes and Ms. K. obviously wants to play it hard into their end for the last fifteen minutes.

The other team is walking back slowly, some sort of mini conference in their goal box.

"Ms. K. says she was just kidding when she told you to score in two minutes..." Janine laughs as we wait. "Tina says if she'd known you were such a showoff she would have asked your mom to come out to our home games earlier in the season."

I raise my eyebrows in response, risk a glance at Tina who gives me a thumbs-up from the sidelines. I have this feeling she knows I'm pissed off but doesn't know why. Her face is still tomato-coloured with an icy sponge of whiteness underneath but she's regained composure and her mouth is set in a rigid, tinny smile. What a can of worms. I don't bother to acknowledge her, but it doesn't matter. Just at that moment, Brad Bellows walks up behind her and tickles her under the ponytail. My sister wriggles in a fit of shivery grace as long thin giggles are peeled from underneath her hard muscled body. At 105, her body is twelve pounds leaner than mine, like a flexible plastic drinking straw, instantly bent at the knees. He whispers something and sucks at her earlobe.

Ms. K. says her name, sharply, and Brad vanishes. We aren't supposed to have guys at the game. Distraction, and all that. Except that I'm the distracted one, and it's not even my boyfriend.

The next thing I know, Ms. K. has sent Tina in. A last-minute change. She is at centre halfback right behind me. She's never played midfield before, so I guess she'll just play it defensive, hammering it hard up to me whenever it comes within spitting distance.

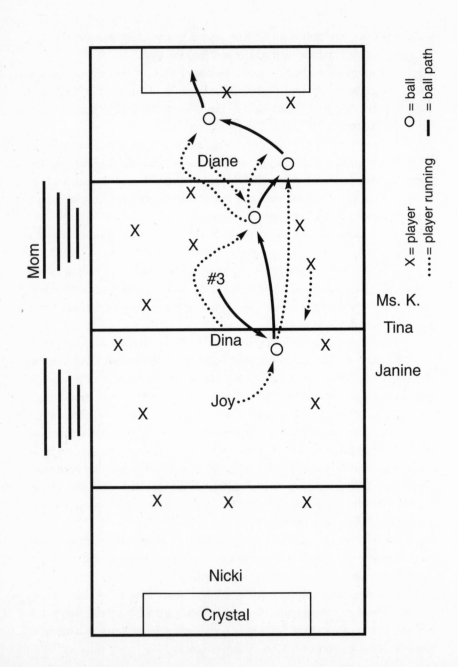

The ref blows the whistle and Number 3 taps it back to Diane who's come up for the pass. She belts it hard.

"Head it! Head it!" I can hear my mother's voice over all the others, as it sails over me.

Tina jumps to catch it in the air off the top of her head. Instead of directing it with her forehead, it pops straight up again. Enough time for the stamp of feet and them to be on us. She and Number 3 are both in the air for the second head but the ref calls it on Number 3 for leaning into Tina, going over her back.

It goes without saying Tina will take the penalty kick. Janine and Joy and I are tit to tit with the defensive line, as Diane's hollering, "Pull it up. Hold them up," wanting to sprint ahead of us before the ball's kicked, so they'll get the offside call.

But we're ready. The whole line of us, moving backwards from the direction we want to go. Tina pops the ball up over all of our heads, as two teams move towards her. Before it even hits ground, we're all turned around again, and sprinting for it.

I can see Janine's got it, and I run about fifteen feet away from her, parallel, waiting for the pass. She's got a player on her, and to keep her from tapping it out of bounds, Janine gives it a nudge with the outside of her foot in my direction. It's too light and before I can react, I see Diane's going to get it. But she's facing their net, and she'll either have to put it back to their goalie—which will give me a chance to rush from this distance—or else she'll have to turn it.

What is happening is faster than thought, but I have time to anticipate every move and make my decisions. That's why I play. Our bodies are like pinballs on this wooden-dry patch of field. You can tilt the game just a bit to your advantage, but if you pick it up too much, you'll forfeit everything. You can feel that spot though, how far you can push it without ruining everything. That invisible groove between thought and instinct. I feel it now, the way I want to slant this game, and I'm already moving to accommodate. I don't know if it's because I know Diane Wells' mindset, or because I've known soccer since grade six. This is what I know: Wells is not going to turn it.

What she actually does is start to run it back to her goalie. I know I can't get a good foot on it, but I can run beside her and hope to make her nervous. She starts leaning heavily on me even though it's slowing her down. I let off a step and while she's off balance, I decide to slide tackle. One little angel on my shoulder says, Go for the ball. The other says, Go for the shins.

The field seems to unfold beneath my burning thigh. The bottom of my cleats hit the ball. Diane pitches over me. Half her weight smashes down in the centre of my chest on spikes. The other half thumps fist first into the dirt. It's a fair play only because I accurately hit the ball, sending it straight to Janine, who's probably at this moment picking a corner of the net to shoot for. Probably. If I could see. If I could breathe.

Pain is the only thing that cancels everything that has come before or after.

I watch the straight line of the field tip into the sky like a dart into a balloon. My ribs and guts have become a cage of shark's incisors to my breath, allowing me to draw in but not expel.

My sister's breathing hits me in a wash of stale saliva, the fine blonde hair on her knees the only thing I can accurately identify.

"Where does it hurt?" she asks and, without waiting for an answer, "Stay down," she says, and "Don't move, Dina."

Somewhere over me, Diane Wells' breathes, "It's not my fault. She did it herself." I feel the sunlight buckling as she stands and bends over me, watching.

"Stand back," Ms. K. commands as she jogs up.

And Diane does. Tina is more reluctant, and after another minute, my chest relents and I can draw the air in again as if I were a human breathing, instead of a fish with a slit in its side.

Ms. K. places a firm hand over my left breast and pushes on my ribs through the fat, feeling each one. Certainly not the way I envisioned the scenario of the first other person to ever feel my breasts. "Tell me when it hurts," she says, and pushing her palm down to the bones she moves from one nub to the other. They hurt on both sides. They all hurt.

"You may have cracked or bruised your ribs," she says, "But you probably just had the wind knocked out of you. Come on, let's get you on your feet, kiddo."

People on the sidelines begin to applaud as Ms. K. and my sister loop my arms around their shoulders and walk me over to the side of the field where my mother is waiting, lidded cup in one hand and the windbreaker off her shoulders to wrap around mine. I've never understood that ritual, why people clap when you acknowledge that you can't keep going.

"Honey..." Mom emphasizes as if it was my first name. She offers me the cup. I can't breathe well enough to sniff it, so I hold my head up and take a small swallow. It's...water. There is some small relief.

We crouch together on the sidelines and watch my sister take my place, moving up from halfback to take the kick. It's a drop ball, since the ref can't assign fault for the injury to either Diane or myself. My sister faces off with my friend/enemy. The ball is dropped approximately between them, and everything could go one way or the other.

If you could pinpoint the crisis before it occurs, you could step back from the play. But now someone else is sent in to play, someone neither good nor bad, but other. And I sit on the sidelines and watch the game go on without me.

The one question you would ask of anyone who has ever hurt you, is why. That's what I would ask, anyway. In spite of the fact that the answer might be as shrill and wordless as a whistle. Why? Why? This is what I would ask my mother, my father, my sister. Diane Wells, just a number on a large playing field.

I feel myself impaled on each breath I try to pull in, and I clutch my stomach with one hand and my heart with the other, as if I could make the pain disappear that easily.

The ball is dropped.

My sister gets the first foot on it, the black-and-white object hurtling straight into the other team's net before the keeper even thinks to move towards it.

THE MOTHERS

I

THE FIRST THING I LEARNED BOTH BACKWARDS AND FORWARDS WAS THE
LORD'S PRAYER.

At Mary Marlies' house in her mother's basement, we held our own youth
group. Her mother supervised us in a sense. Everyone got a chair and one
would be marked on its underside with a cross. Like a birthday party's X,
whoever had the lucky chair would get a prize, a bible picture postcard of
the misty Virgin Mary or Baby Jesus. And we would sing, "Jesus Loves Me,"
"Little ones to Him belong. They are weak, but He is strong..." and say the
Lord's Prayer. But in Mary's bathroom after the meeting, Amy Simpson
would swing her legs while she peed; it took a long time for her to get the
pee going sometimes, and Mary would pretend the bathtub ledge was a
tightrope, teetering along while we sang quietly, "Jason loves me, this I
know..." after Jason Pinto in our class, with reasons that changed depending on whether he had stolen our hats at recess or tagged us in the gym.
Then, abruptly, sometimes mid-verse, Mary would jump down and say as
earnestly as a seven-year-old can "Stop it!" as if she couldn't bear the blas-
phemy, as if the whole thing had been mine and Amy's idea.

"Group" was mainly Mary's project though. More than her mother's, and it became very important that we be there every Monday. At school in the morning, she would begin by making promises, allusions to "Oh, what will the prize be today?" and that it was something special, very special, maybe a glow-in-the-dark Jesus nightlight that plugged in and everything. When it turned out to be another postcard, Amy and I fumed secretly in the bathroom without Mary, me running the taps to make her pee, and she saying, "If you learn the Lord's Prayer backwards and forwards, isn't that kind of like the opposite? Putting it in reverse?" Right then we set about learning the prayer word for word entirely backwards, the way the boys in our class said their older brothers played their albums in reverse to hear messages from the dead. Whenever Mary promised an extra special prize for Group, Amy and I would look at each other and silently mouth the last line backwards from all the way across the classroom, our secret curse on Mary: *Nem-ha, reve dna reve rof. Yrolg eht dna rewop eht.*

So of course, it's no wonder when she finally caught on, she promised to fill my pillowcase with spider's eggs. She said they would hatch out while I was sleeping and crawl all over me and eat me alive. I started having nightmares and wouldn't go to bed. My mother decided to put an end to my religious education after that.

2

ALL MOTHERS' ANGELS HAUNT THEM.

Later, Mary Marlies' mother became a bona fide leader at the church for a group called "Keepers," which I guess meant keeping faith or keeping the light, although it always seemed sort of a shady name to me, like keeping secrets or something. I never went, but it was basically their church's equivalent of Brownies. All through elementary school Mary Marlies gave out Christmas cards with the Virgin Mother and the little baby Jesus after the rest of us had given out cards depicting Santa and Rudolph in ridiculous situations, or better yet, opted to give out candy or nothing at all.

"Don't you think it's creepy?" Amy asked me in grade five, just after the holidays, as I was helping her and her mom un-decorate. She pulled the cards down off the wall.

"Amy..." her mother warned, "Christmas is about more than a new pair of leg warmers." Or some reference to some other now outdated garment or game that Amy had recently received.

"I know," Amy nodded, over her shoulder mouthing to me, *Nem-ha, reve dna reve rof.* "It's just that they've got all those pictures and figurines through the whole house, and the bathtub Madonna with spotlights, and it's all about Jesus loves the little children, and Mrs. Marlies can't stand Mary or her sisters."

"Amy!" her mother warned. "She's got four kids, she's got her hands full, that's all. Of course, she's not that bright, they're not the best-off family in town, but they manage." Mrs. Simpson spoke in that low, all-knowing mother voice. That judge-not-lest-ye-be-judged voice. It didn't sound a whole lot like she was disagreeing with Amy, but as if she had to qualify the statement in case there was a God who was listening who might damn us all for picking on those who were less fortunate. She packed the ornaments carefully into the white plastic tray. "God is in all of us," Mrs. Simpson said, carefully wrapping the tree-top angel in layers of white tissue paper. "Even on our bad days, we carry Him deep down inside." When she put it like that, I couldn't help but imagine God as a half-formed child, yellowish and illuminated, swimming in a sac of red fluid like the foetus in the anti-abortion literature that I'd seen.

Like most of the families in our neighbourhood, the Simpsons were occasional Catholics, dutiful but reserved. Amy rolled her eyes discreetly, and began sorting the cards into keepsakes and throwaways. Mother Mary was first into throwaway.

I knew what Amy was getting at. Life at the Marlies house held a hauntedness. Their daily rituals were as far from grace as we could imagine at that time in our lives. There was never any milk in the fridge, and we didn't ask for snacks when we went there. Mary was so thin that if you punchbuggied her arm, no matter how friendly a tap, she would bruise clear through to the other side, almost as if there was no blood in her. The basement was full of dolls with their eyes penned out, and everything smelled faintly of pee.

Despair was like a flickering spectre kneeling on their living room floor in front of the television—she could be seen when the daylight reached a certain patch of the carpet if the channel was changed at just that moment. A blue and gold hologram Jesus in a gilt-looking plastic frame hung in the alcove beside the front door, and in every room He carried His cross. "Don't go down in our basement alone. The stairs will open up and you'll fall into Hell," Mary had once told us solemnly. "I mean it. There's ghosts down there."

Mrs. Marlies spent her days lounging in the house watching soap operas in a long black sheer bathrobe with her hair in tight pink foam curlers. Several times when we'd come home after school with Mary we'd caught her that way, 3:30 in the afternoon and still not dressed. She'd jump up immediately, point at the vacuum sitting in the middle of the room, and croon, "Mary, give me a hand. I started to do the rugs but I think I put my back out. I was just taking a rest to see if the pain would go away." We'd look embarrassed that her mother was still in her housecoat and visibly half-naked. Mary would stall. And after about three minutes Mrs. Marlies would yell, "You stupid brats! You never lift a finger to help me! Your father's going to be home in an hour and there's going to be all hell if this Goddamn house isn't clean, Mary!"

At 4:30 Mary's father would come home and regardless of whether the carpet had been cleaned or not, it would be, "This place looks like a shithouse! Mary, what are all your friends doing here? Who said you could have them over? What are you doing playing with that? You're in the middle of the floor, taking up the whole room." He'd make a lousy demonstration of pretending to swerve around Mary, nearly always managing to step on her hand on the way past. "Well, get out of the *fucking* way, then," he'd say as she yelped. The word carried more weight than a backhand.

Mary's teenage sister, Josephine, would come into the doorway, lean her whip-thin arm on her hip and watch as we quickly detached from the scene. The younger sisters, Sarah and Ruth, popped heads from the bedrooms down the hall, stood picking noses, then scuttled out of sight like cockroaches. Mrs. Marlies would send us home as politely as possible under the circumstances. She had to get supper ready, and then drive over to excercise class or the church.

Even then, I had this image of Mrs. Marlies waking up next to her husband and praying that she'd never married him, never had kids, never had any reason to pray.

My first exposure to sex was at the Marlies house. It was Mary's birthday and we couldn't very well get out of it because they'd rented a VCR for the evening. So we were part obligated, and part tempted. About two hours after we'd bedded down on the living room floor, and pssted and giggled and done all of that, Mary fell asleep, and then everyone else followed suit. Except for me and Amy. She was sharing my blankets and we were quietly taking turns drawing words on each other's backs with our fingers: *Jason -L- Janie* and *Jason -L- Amy.*

Mr. Marlies came out of the bedroom, and the hall light came on. He walked into the dining room that stood between the hall and the den, where we were.

"Eddy?" Mrs. Marlies called from the far end of the house, a hushed urgency in her voice that even at that age I somehow knew not to mistake for desire. "Come back to bed."

He stood in the double doorway with his hands on his hips. He was wearing a pair of blue briefs exactly like the kind my dad had, except he filled them out more. "Who's still awake?" he said. He said it, he didn't whisper, almost as if he was bidding anyone who was asleep to wake up. I felt Amy freeze behind me, and I lay still, not even daring to shut my eyes. "Who wants to play hide-and-seek with me?"

I didn't know what he meant, but I knew what he meant. Amy's fingernails bit into my bicep. He was looking at her, what he could see of her, her blonde curls on the pillow. She was the pretty one, the girly one, and we both knew it. She squeezed until I could feel the circulation cut off and I knew if he came to take her, he'd have to tear her off of me first.

He turned and walked away. "Don't let the bed bugs bite," he said gruffly over his shoulder with a bit of a snicker.

Amy and I didn't say a word. Then or ever. She pulled the blanket over our heads and I turned over and faced her. I pulled her face down into my chest and held her around the shoulders. She curled her knees up to her stomach and tucked her feet between my thighs. They were ice cold and I didn't fall asleep until the digital clock on the VCR said 5:15.

I dreamed of a centipede with one hundred feet, and on each foot an inside out sock. He was curled up on my pillow when I opened my eyes. "Wh-wh-wh-*what* are you looking at?" he said in a voice like the caterpillar in *Alice in Wonderland*. He slid off my pillow and charged into my mouth. I jolted awake. Old threats never die; I still hated bugs.

Amy's hair had fallen on my face, and her fingers were crushed palm-up underneath me digging into my ribs. The light fell through the rust-brown sheer drapes and the beige carpet looked like it'd been stained with blood in blotchy flower-shaped patches. Mary was sitting up already picking at an old scab on her elbow.

"I don't feel good," I told her. I got up and went to the bathroom, made a big production of flushing the toilet several times and running the water. Amy and I were ten years old. We'd watched *Sixteen Candles* and made it through the night. When I came out, I went straight to the phone and called my mother to come get us.

Sheila Shepherd's mother didn't have the God-fixation but their house was just as creepy when we went there. Mrs. Shepherd worked nights at the factory and was obsessed with dogs. She had a ten-year-old Scottie named Jonas, which strangely, was also Sheila's older brother's name. It might have made sense if the dog had been named by Jonas himself, but it wasn't. Mrs. Shepherd named it. Both of the kids hated the dog. The boy Jonas used to fill the dog Jonas's water dish with Sprite, root beer, or beer, hoping that the dog would get gas and their mother would decide it was too stinky to have around the house. But the dog merely belched and lapped up more. Sheila used to steal the blue ribbons off it and keep them in her desk at school. One day she pulled them out and counted them in front of us on lunch hour.

"This is how much my mother loves the dog," she said. "Three hundred and fifty-seven, three hundred and fifty-eight, three hundred and fifty-nine ribbons in the past ten months."

We were impressed. It was a lot of love, obviously, to keep replacing ribbons when they went missing, as if there was a never-ending supply. We liked dogs, frankly, and almost understood Sheila's mother's obsession better than we did Sheila's.

The problem for Sheila was that she never saw her mother. Hadn't seen her, in fact, in the ten months that she had been taking the dog's ribbons. Her mother had switched shifts, working opposite hours from her father. She now worked from three in the afternoon until midnight. Sometimes, Sheila said, she stayed up and saw her father off to work, and then she could see her mother for a few minutes. But other times, she would lie half-awake, overhearing her mother talking to Jonas, the Scottie, in the kitchen, opening the refrigerator to get him milk or treats. Or she would hear her inviting him into bed with her, brushing his fur, she'd cluck and fuss, and make cutesy noises in his ears. Once, Sheila said, she asked her mother if she could iron her clothes and lay them out for her for the morning. "You're ten years old, Sheila," her mother apparently replied. "You're not a baby." Jonas, the second Jonas, was her perpetual child.

When we went for Sheila's birthday party, we saw the walls full of professional photographs of Jonas. Jonas with a ball, Jonas with his bows, Jonas with his trainer and Mrs. Shepherd. Over the couch where our parents had hung our school photos, Mrs. Shepherd had only Jonas. On the fridge there were three pictures of the family. A baby picture of Sheila's brother, a baby picture of Sheila, and a picture of Sheila at nine months crawling across the floor towards a startled Jonas and his food bowl.

Jonas sat in Mrs. Shepherd's lap at the table. He was wearing a fresh blue ribbon. When we sang "Happy Birthday dear Sheila," Mrs. Shepherd manipulated Jonas' paws to wave at her, "Happy Birthday says Jonas," Mrs. Shepherd intoned loudly over top of all of us. Mr. Shepherd snorted, went to the fridge and got out a bottle of Blue. He didn't seem the type to put up with it, and it was obvious that he adored Sheila. He kissed her, and he teased us, and he'd bought her the Michael Jackson album and a silky red jacket with the name of the nearest rollerskating rink emblazoned across the back in gold letters. Mrs. Shepherd gave her a hand-knitted cardigan with pictures of dogs on the pockets and the back.

Sheila on-purpose/by-accident left it in the gym at school and it got thrown into the Lost and Found box in the office until a third-grade girl, a kid from the geared-to-income-housing, wound up claiming it later that spring. When Sheila saw her with it, she followed the girl home from school, beat her up, and took the sweater and hung it in her own closet never to be worn again.

Jonas was put to sleep the next year. Mrs. Shepherd didn't get another dog until Sheila left home at fourteen to move in with her boyfriend who was out of school and worked at the Shell Station. I would see Mrs. Shepherd out on walks with the Shih Tzu, which she'd adorned with red ribbons, and called Sheila.

3

UNCONDITIONAL LOVE IS ONLY POSSIBLE IN SOMEONE ELSE'S SITUATION.

By the time we'd all hit thirteen, we were ready to do some serious mother swapping. It had become obvious to each of us that our mothers had certain idiosyncracies that we were fated to inherit.

All of the stereotypical teenage traits, we saw emerging not in us, but in our mothers. It was as if they were growing larger in front of our eyes, their bodies became bulbous and sexual, bizarre and foreign. Their voices seemed to change.

Suddenly, we were aware of them in ways we had never been: how they laughed, the voices they used on the telephone, their atrocious taste in music, the frequency with which they shaved their legs, their clothing choices to *our* functions and their fussiness over what we deemed age-appropriate clothing for ourselves. Our awareness was acute; when they walked into rooms, we could *smell* them.

If any sense was going to come out of this, we knew it was up to us. Our mothers were hopeless. Their wills were out of control and it was our job to lay down the law. For the sake of our individual houses as well as our united social well-being.

For some girls in my class at school, there was an intense courting of guilt, and sexual exploration was the main means to exceed parental expectation: the reward/punishment of new attentions—shame, shame and extra Sunday servings of shame. The rest of us used unspoken, unwritten codes of silence regarding these matters, including outright avoidance, while still carrying an abstract sense of duty to the family, primarily to maintain a certain level of attractiveness without high-heeled boots or excessive eyeliner.

But even at the time, we knew that these were only the basics to surviving our parents. The contradictory morals in our individual houses were as different and unnoticed as wallpaper. We knew the patterns without looking, had traced them in boredom during our younger years, then stopped seeing them, in fact, forgot they were even there...until our friends came by and began hanging about our houses while our parents were out, commenting on everything from the refrigerator contents to the bedroom closets. Everything was suddenly about what we had or didn't have. Frozen pizza or canned Alfaghetti, no-name products or brand labels, board games or video games, pads or tampons. And none of it, not any, had to do with our fathers. Everything was our mother's faults.

Almost as much as we categorized each other, we categorized each other's mothers. Mrs. Marlies was a sulky pushover who let Mr. Marlies tramp over everything. Mrs. Shepherd...well, we never went to the Shepherd's by that point. Mrs. Simpson was the cool mom who was willing to drive us places and let us meet up with boys, never failing to remind us of our feminine power and, of course, the best way to maintain power (abstinence). And my mother, Mrs. Blasé, who was just liberal enough to be passable among my friends, but still too firm to be a favourite, and just never quite, well, Mrs. Simpson.

To me, Mrs. Simpson was the small town version of sophisticated. She was in the process of divorcing, and though money was tight, Mrs. Simpson still had subscriptions to magazines like *Cosmopolitan*, *Chatelaine* and, okay, also the less elegant but ever popular *Woman's Day*. She dieted and had disco dresses stashed in the back of her closet. She was the first mom I knew with the guts to go ultra-short with her hair and ultra-heavy with her makeup. She was a fashion-plate for the mid-80s—her bangs blonde-silver spikes, and her blush like racing stripes. Mrs. Simpson never complained about the divorce even when she and Amy moved into a one-bedroom duplex apartment and had to share a room. Instead she would say, "Well, we just have to think of *our future* now," as if without Mr. Simpson, she and Amy had become a couple. She consumed cigarettes like candy and talked about all those big topics like God and Love in the same breath. Issues we skirted at my house. She was at once a woman of frivolity and of great strength.

If there is unconditional love in this world—something the talk shows were fond of discussing at that time, though they never came to this conclusion—it undoubtedly occurs only between girls and their friends' mothers. And only for a very brief and beautiful period of time. Through all of grade seven, I wanted to live at the Simpsons', and by some unfathomable twist, Amy wanted to live at my house. She said her mother was an old cheese doodle, and at least mine was reasonable.

Is it a terrible thing for a daughter to say? I never loved my mother the same way I loved Mrs. Simpson.

All of the horror movies at that time were about bad mothers. Or whores, of course, who never go out of fashion, at least not in movies. But bad mothers were really in. I'm not sure it occurred to us that there could be bad daughters.

I spent every weekend at Amy's house, and didn't realize what it was doing to my mother until I called one afternoon to say I wouldn't be home for supper. My mother wouldn't talk to me. She'd made roast beef. I didn't find out this reason until later. She just handed the phone to my father. I could hear her crying in the background. I'd never heard my mother cry before.

My dad didn't say anything for a minute. Then he said the same thing I'd always heard my friends' mothers say about their husbands. "Your mother works hard. So that you will have things." He didn't sound angry, but point of fact. "Come home."

The sad thing is, that wasn't the moment I knew I couldn't live at the Simpsons' forever. I didn't figure that out for another half a year.

Amy and I were in grade eight. We were hanging out under The Bridge with some kids from the school on the other side of town. We weren't supposed to be hanging out with them, and especially weren't supposed to be under The Bridge. The Bridge was one of three, we said to each other, and when our parents said, "Don't hang out under The Bridge," we decided they must have meant one of the other two. Especially since this particular bridge was the closest to our neighbourhood, we said to ourselves, it could therefore not be as bad as the other two. Still, we knew, that not even This Bridge should we be under.

But we were under it. A couple of the guys were drinking beer from cans, but we weren't. We had gone so Amy could meet The Boy I Was Secretly In Love With. In fact, Amy had just gotten her first French kiss from The Boy I Was Secretly In Love With, and she was standing around inhaling air like it was in short supply. Since she seemed to be having a hard time recovering her lung capacity after he'd put his tongue in her mouth, The Boy decided it might help if she took a drag off his cigarette. Which she was doing just as we heard her mother's voice.

"Oh shit," I said.

Amy jabbed the cigarette at me, and she would have looked completely innocent if she hadn't started coughing just as her mother's wooden-soled sandals came clanking down the metal stairs onto the grate beside us.

"Amy," her mother said in that voice mothers use when you know they'd rather slap you than speak to you. There was a long, shocked pause. "Let's go," she said finally, with only a glance at the cigarette I was holding amateurishly between my index finger and thumb.

Amy didn't say anything, just started up the stairs ahead of her mother towards the car in lot. I took a step forward to follow, assuming I was going to get it too. But my adopted mother continued without another look at me. "I'm taking Amy home," she said over her shoulder, and I listened to the clank clank clank as she climbed the bridge stairs with her back to me.

I realized as soon as she was gone that I was still naively holding Amy and The Boy's cigarette.

"Wanna finish it with me?" he asked with a smirk that implied he might have meant more than the cigarette.

I looked at the long hair and the pair of tight white jeans that had first drawn my attention. Somehow they didn't seem so attractive anymore. "No thanks," I said and gave the cigarette back, and left.

I thought that when I got home my parents might already know where we'd been. But Mrs. Simpson hadn't called. I was disappointed. Amy told me at school the next day that her mom didn't feel it was her business. I lived at their house three days out of seven, but I wasn't her *business*.

It was only then that I wished I'd at least stayed and finished things with The Boy.

4

SOMETIMES STRANGER THINGS ARE BORN.

The first babies began a couple of years later. Friends from grade school like Mary and Sheila, and acquaintances we'd made in high school. Their bellies swelled up and we watched them transform from a distance. Become round and awkward. While people tried to say nice things about growing up quickly, taking responsibility for one's actions (we seemed to be living in the anti-abortion capital of Canada), and having that motherly glow, we saw only ugly blue sweatshirts and old pink genie pants. In a juvenile way, pregnancy was like a proof of purchase. Though you could cut it out from the box and mail it in for a prize, we were old enough to understand that a) if the box was still full, the cereal would go stale, and b) such prizes never have value. Why other girls our age couldn't see this, we never knew.

In the span of a summer our world was suddenly divided into two camps: girls who did, and girls who didn't.

Amy was still in my camp, but she kept sneaking over to the other camp when I wasn't around. She told me wild stories of The Gorgeous Guy she was seeing, and how she let him put his hands up her shirt. And then her shorts. And then, and then.

"I thought we should use *something*," she kept confiding. "But I can't go to the doctor. I heard that unless you're sixteen, you need your mother's permission to get The Pill."

"But you have to use something!" I said emphatically.

"You want to buy condoms for me? My aunt works at the drugstore, and it's not like she doesn't know who he is!"

"Oh my God. How many times without a...?" I gestured vaguely with my hand, as if my tongue had turned to rubber and couldn't flap out the word.

"You sound like my mother," she said. Then she wiped her hand across her face and admitted, "Five times, but he pulled out."

"Five times! What are you going to do?"

"Pray." There was not a trace of sarcasm.

In grade eleven, Amy started bussing to the Catholic high school, which was somehow considered "cooler" in spite of the lower availability of birth control information. Either prayer actually worked for her as a method, or she convinced someone else to buy condoms for The Guy. Or, by that point, he had his driver's licence, and took her to some other doctor's office or some other pharmacy. Or maybe he was replaced by some other Gorgeous Guy who would.

The pain was like something living, chewing on my womb for breakfast. My stomach was in knots. I could only clutch at it, untuck my shirt to hide the undone top of my jeans, which otherwise formed a tight band across the aching. I had a spare for second period, and would slouch down across a couple of chairs in the cafeteria while my friends played a lusty round of Go Fish, wherein each card held the secret significance of some Guy or Other who the players might have crushes on.

Love was a non-stop entertainment. Everything indicated a fuck: pop tabs pulled all the way off in one rip, cars on the highway with one headlight out, apple stems twisted to the alphabet song and snapping off on the letter of the right boy's name. I was seventeen years old, and I had graduated to the other camp. *Jason loves me this I know...* Except that Jason Pinto had become a dealer and a burnout. The Guy's name was actually John, in this case, and I didn't know if he loved me, even though he'd told me he did, several times. More important, I had grown truly tired of belonging to Camp Virgin. He was a fun guy, and though not altogether Gorgeous, I was certain I was not the first girl with whom he had acquiesced. I liked him. Whether or not I loved him was not the issue at hand, and in the hour between school's out and the five o'clock whistle when his parents came home he was too hurried and excited to ask for declarations.

The condom had not been stored in his wallet for months on end, had been checked for punctures, had been kept away from heat sources, sharp objects such as keys, jewellery and fingernails. We'd both read all instructions, probably several times, at home locked in our separate bedrooms or bathrooms, months in advance of the day we might each find someone who would want to use one. It was the same way I had started reading the tampon instructions from my mother's box in the bathroom cupboard the day I turned twelve, even though it would be another year and a half before I had any use for them. But the condom was not 100% effective, and we knew this before we used it.

The thing inside me was not a baby. It was a disease. One the doctors named Chlamydia, as they worked at getting it out. In this case, tongs were not necessary. A prescription would do.

My primary doctor was a woman my mother's age, and I might have been grateful for a female doctor if she hadn't resembled Nurse Ratched. I had just watched the movie in conjunction with reading *One Flew Over the Cuckoo's Nest* for my grade twelve English independent study project. I could tell right away that the doctor had a low opinion of me, because she asked me the same questions twice, as if she thought I hadn't told her the truth the first time.

There is nothing as definite as the sound of rubber gloves snapping on wrists for striking fear into a teenage girl. The sound of the wheels squeaking on the chair as it is rolled into place. The heat of the light at the end of the table turned upon the most private part of you. Nothing as frightening except the pseudo-sermon that comes after clothes have been put back on.

Until then, I had hoped to avoid pregnancy at all costs. Now, so far as Ratched could discern, my ovaries were still intact and my fallopian tubes hadn't been damaged, much. That little word caught on my ear, and the fog closed in.

"Of more concern to me..." Ratched said, folding her hands in her lap in a way that bothered me immensely since it indicated there was more to come when I was already quite ready to flee the facility "...is that you understand that the people to whom these things happen tend to face problems again...unless they take precautions."

What I wanted to say was, "Submit Exhibit A for evidence." To have the door swing open, and a uniformed marshal come forth with a manilla envelope. In it, the sodden condom from that afternoon several months before.

What I said was, "Yes. I understand perfectly."

My mother was waiting for me in the parking lot. "Who did you see this time?" she asked when I climbed up into the truck. She was wearing a flannel jacket of my father's, the cuffs rolled back. Her hands were like brown leather mitts on the wheel. Her face, suddenly filled in with diverging lines, was heavier around the eyes and mouth than I had noticed before. She had grown with me. Her tousled honey hair was whitening as the snow fell behind her outside the fogged window in the milky midafternoon winter light. She was getting older as I watched.

When I told her, she said, "Oh, I like that doctor! I saw her once. I liked going to a woman gyno. She's very progressive and very good!"

My mother had been very nice about all of it. Nicer than any other mother would have been, I thought. She nodded her head, and asked only the questions she needed the answers to. So this time, I didn't contradict her. I nodded when what I wanted was to curl into a foetal position and cry. My mother started the engine and waited for me to fasten my seat belt like always. I did. With a cold metallic click, it slid into place, and caught. She was still my mother; I was not a mother. But something had irreversibly changed.

5

IMAGINE THE MOTHERS GATHERED IN ONE ROOM.

Imagine them, as I did at that moment. Imagine them as a group, a cross-section of society, a clear colour photograph in a text book: a semicircle of women of all backgrounds, all family situations, all incomes. A demographic, from the clothes they wear to the things they carry. The flat yet feminine shoes, the handbags full of bandages and peppermints, the blazers, sweaters, or sweatshirts. Imagine them young. Imagine them old. Imagine yourself among them. Imagine yourself absent.

Imagine them, as in a dream, the crazy shapes they make against the light source you can not quite identify. The secrets they might tell, leaning into one another, big bellied, big breasted, pear-shaped or as yet unformed. Their voices low, murmuring of blood, pain, patience.

Imagine The Mothers gathered together, murmuring, murmuring...

Imagine one mother. The image of a mother. The Madonna. The virgin mother. A pale blue and blonde postcard with hands clasped. Imagine the light behind her. How singular of virtue. Shining and praying. How alone she seems, how lonely.

MEASUREMENT LISTINGS IN THE CATALOGUE OF MEMORY

THERE IS SOMETHING both comforting and unsettling about knowing your death is arriving.

Leigh's mother is making lists. Things Purchased. Things Still to be Bought. Uncertain People. Miscellaneous Items. Dinner Menu. Card List. People to Call.

They are not unlike the lists she made when Leigh's Grampy died. People to Call. Funeral Details. Expenses. Estate Details. Thank-you Card List. Etc.

Leigh is sitting opposite her mother making a list of her own. In her lap the Christmas catalogue lies open to the household section, as there are very few passable clothing items for someone of Leigh's sensibilities. If anyone had told Leigh that she would still be coming home after all these years to choose her own presents and mark them out by code number at her mother's insistence, even as a little girl Leigh would have told them to go dunk their heads.

Leigh's life can be divided neatly in her mind. Things That Happened Before I Jumped in the River. Things That Happened After the River. These last three years, she thinks of it with an almost ritualistic fascination, a mix of horror and nostalgia. The river, like a tight passage of dark skin, broken. The canal between her childhood and her adult life.

Leigh wonders if her mother has another set of lists tucked inside the desk drawer in her bedroom. Lists for her own funeral. Her mother's, that is. Leigh's mother's lists for her own funeral, set conveniently on top in a marked envelope so that Leigh and her father, Hank, will find them as soon as it has happened. Maybe right there on top of the rose leather address book her mother has continued to use and update these last thirty years. As long as Leigh can remember.

Before the river incident, Leigh had a premonition. Not long before, maybe ten or twenty minutes. Just before she and her friends drove to the riverfront. It wasn't a planned thing, understand. Just something that happened that she knew was going to happen. That somehow, even though they had no reason to go and no one had suggested it, Neil would turn the car and drive down that way. That someone would say the thing she knew they would say. Were supposed to say. The thing that would set her off. Nothing her mother hadn't said before. And then, that Leigh would make an excuse to get out of the car so she could jump into the river. Just as she was supposed to. It was pulling her. Closer and closer. Really. Pulling her in.

It sounds so premeditated, she might think it was. If she wasn't herself, that is. It would be easy to think this was her way of avoiding responsibility for her actions. For plunging into a frozen river, and Gage winding up vaulting the rail two seconds later to get a hold on her. Her nearly getting them both killed in the dark seamless silver ribbon of water, holding hands with ice chunks, unable to pull themselves out. But the truth is, Leigh's truth: it was her birthday; she was menstruating; there was a full moon; there was water; she was pulled.

It's true, she had those few minutes in which to stop herself. Before they drove down to the water. Those moments of knowing. Yet there was nothing she could do. It was one of those surreal yet ordinary revelations—like looking at the telephone and knowing it was about to ring and then, of course, it ringing. She could have opted not to pick it up. But it was ringing nonetheless. Just like she knew it would. Still, she sometimes wonders if her will had been stronger, could she have mentally turned the entire car and headed them all in some other direction?

She pauses over the coral-coloured gravy boat. Even though she is a vegetarian. She writes down the code. Its shape is exquisite. Squat, bulbous, feminine.

Her mother is looking over her shoulder. Deborah, as Leigh has taken to calling her since the diagnosis. She knows her father has noticed, that he thinks Leigh cruel—her way of distancing herself before it happens—always gives her that one eyebrow sliding down, a grey black needle from the spool of his head towards his eye. And then he closes his eyes into slitted buttonholes and creases.

The truth is Leigh is beginning to see her mother as more. As a woman, rather than the vessel by which she was freighted into the world. As more than a set of washcloth thumbs and napkined lips, a coil of telephone vocal chords, a supply of bandages and dollar bills. Deborah. Disappointment, humour, hope, anger, appetite, will. A life. A life, but only glimpsed as it passes. She sees her mother's life only as her mother prepares for its ending.

"Here," Deborah says, turning the pages as rapidly as she is able, "you have lots of kitchen things. You need some nice clothes. Something you can wear for that big interview." Leigh hasn't lined up any big interview as of yet. She works part-time in a small bar on Cass Avenue in Detroit. If she dressed up she'd never make it from her car to the door. The rest of her time is spent doing web design from home. She doesn't even meet with her clients most of the time, they come by referral from other small-scale businesses, and if she does meet with them, they cater to that eighteen to thirtysomething educated hip demographic anyway and the frumpier she looks probably the better.

She needs clothes for the funeral. She needs to be prepared for what they know is going to happen.

It is as though the ten minutes before her own brush with death has stretched itself out over the span of nine months. As if before she jumped, she'd had time to see a doctor, and the doctor had told her what she'd already known, that yes, indeed, it was inevitable: the dark water was about to pull her in. As if she'd had time to meditate on the details of all that would follow her jump, time to plan who should be contacted, who should be told before and who after. Yet regardless of the advance knowledge, the events would still play out the same way, a black loop of video tape, or round shaky reels of film spliced to repeat. The telephone endlessly ringing.

Deborah picks it up. Deborah talks into the receiver, and Leigh listens to her mother's voice from this end, the uncanny closeness as she hears the tone changes reserved for telephone conversations, the ones she is usually on the other end for instead of in the same room. But she is here. She is still alive. Her mother is still alive. Planning for Christmas, and not her own wake, yet.

Leigh looks at the outfit her mother has turned to. Ankle Length Straight-Cut Skirt with drawstring waist, rustproof steel-tipped baubles. 50% Cotton, 50% Polyester. Back pockets. Side slits. Khaki only. Sizes XS, S, M, L, XL, XXL. Leigh flips to the size guide a few pages back, and realizes with chagrin that she will have to order L in spite of the fact that she has always been an S or an M, and even then, petite in length. She hates the way the sizes change each season. She should be able to order 28", 28" for her whole life, shouldn't she? Nice and simple. Instead of having to match numbers and letters to fashion model eating disorders.

"That would be wonderful," her mother is saying into the telephone. It's one of those old rotary phones that are considered retro. Except that Leigh's parents don't know they're trendy again. They still have this one from 1980 because they didn't like the electronic "ring" of the one they put in upstairs.

Leigh flips back to the blouse and blazer her mother wants to buy for her. Realizes the problem with the skirt sizing is because the skirt is a younger style, meant for the Canadian equivalent of "juniors"; women who are at least ten years younger than Leigh. Women who are still girls.

The blouse on the other hand, is sized for women-sized women. High Necked Eggshell Lace Blouse, invisible back zipper, attached camisole. Bust sizes 32, 34, 36, 38, 40, 42, 44. Easier, Leigh thinks. Men's Style Jacket, double-breasted, double back slit, shoulder pads. 60% Rayon 30% Wool 10% Polyester. Dry clean only. Available Black, Heather Grey, Ecru, Loden, Plum, Fuschia. Bust sizes etc etc. Leigh wonders if Loden will be a slight shade different than Khaki. Always better to go with black, she decides. She surveys the outfit with great skepticism. The pockets probably are just stitched on slips of material for fashion, and the shoulder pads she'd better be able to cut out without ruining the lining. It's no Betsey Johnson, but as her mother says goodbye to Aunt Ann, Leigh writes down the numbers. To make her mother happy. She can live with it.

What Leigh wants though, what she really wants is the coral gravy boat. Because her mother knows she doesn't need it. Because Leigh can't cook anything but dry pasta with canned sauce. She adds fresh garlic and bell peppers to feel gourmet. Soon, Leigh can have her mother's gravy boat, a blue willow china one, originally her grandmother's. But the blue willow looks like her grandmother, not her mom. And Leigh wants to know her mother would buy this just because Leigh wants it. As if it could compensate for all the early years when her parents bought her boxes of chocolate almonds, Precious Moments figurines, bottles of Electric Youth, and Gap sweaters after it had become obvious she was an anti-corporation, Debbie-Gibson-despising, lacto-intolerant atheist.

"A gravy boat. You don't eat meat," Deborah says, when Leigh hands her the list.

It's nice to know her mother finally gets her. Leigh wonders if she'll indulge the whim.

What Gage and Neil and Maggie don't know is that it's never left Leigh's mind. Every day she has thought about the river incident. The moments before, when she felt like the world was spinning at a standstill, waiting to ring, and the moments when it happened. The water, with her body like a needle plunging into the unwound bolt of thick black wool.

What she remembers most clearly was that feeling of having made it. Never, in the waiting or the during, was there fear. That only came after. She has a vague recollection of her arms flying up when she reached the rail and flew over it, like a runner crossing the finish line and breaking the tape. A strange sense of victory.

She wonders if this is what Deborah will feel. The difference, of course, is that Deborah's death is real. Her exit quieter. None of the hoopla and heroics. For now, the wheelchair. Later just the bed, the breathing breathing breathing slowly stitching itself out, until that loose end on the spool finally flips free, leaving the wooden bobbin body. Deborah's thread passing through Leigh's eye. The mother and the daughter. Leigh's body— the needle on the machine, still pumping frantically up and down into the cloth—will keep stitching after the thread is gone.

These are not the first tears, but they feel it, as they always do, with their rawness. Like relatives when they are coming for dinner, their long-awaited arrival, and then something else needs doing and something else, and somehow by the time they're at the door it's not quite an expected entrance. But unlike Leigh's relatives, her tears don't come in carloads. They come one by one, without hugs or kisses. Alone, in the shower. The only private place in her parents' house. Her father's house, soon.

After the river, things changed. Leigh began the slow progression towards adulthood. At the time, the changes she made seemed almost insignificant, small gestures without a lot of movement or force to propel them. Sure, she'd hung on with Gage for a while longer; in the afternoons they still drank tea and did laundry together, at night they still got drunk and made love. There were still outbursts of juvenile overindulgence. She fucked around, but there was always that. And then one day, there was something else, something that had been missing all through those twentysomething escapades. Guilt. Gravity. A sense of being weighted down. That to come back up she had to let go of everyone she had loved. At first, she'd held on harder, reached out for more and more, that ever distant hand that would pull her out of herself.

But all the while, she was treading. Making those slow motions that would lead her. Keeping a steady job, even if only at the bar. Putting the money away. Paying off her debts. Buying the car, the computer, her own bed. Taking the Web courses. Hanging out in places where she could actually hear people talk. Having conversations without having to talk about herself. Those kinds of things.

The bar changed her. She was suddenly on the other side, watching the young girls behaving as she had a million times before. Dragging each other around for secret and meaningful consultations. Things that Leigh knew meant a great deal more when you were the person saying it rather than overhearing it.

But mostly, if she had to pinpoint the biggest change... It was moving across the river, from Windsor to Detroit. Leaving her parents and her friends sitting, there, just slightly long distance, on the other side.

With her Christmas money, Leigh is planning to get another tattoo. Maybe. After her first, she described it honestly to her mother as "a vibrator with teeth." Her mother shuddered at the description, and Leigh now wishes she had said, "a modern-day form of needlepoint." How else to explain this physical symbol, this pattern woven onto the body?

Every year her mother tries to take her to church. Every year Leigh refuses. In her high school days, they had raucous arguments that ended with Leigh slamming doors and playing the Ramones' "We're A Happy Family" on volume nine, always nine because that was the line, if she took it one notch higher her father would go to the fuse box and shut her off.

In those days, Leigh would eventually apologize to her mother, and in turn, her mother would bribe Leigh into submissively attending on Christmas Eve, either by getting her drunk or by giving her extra Christmas money. In her mid-twenties, Leigh continued to argue her not-going stance mostly for the fun of it, not giving in regardless of the prizes or sums her mother might bid.

"Mom," Leigh would say, "What if I asked you to go to a pro-choice rally? If I begged you and told you it was really important to me, and that you would be disgracing me in front of my peers if you didn't come? Would you come?"

"Hey Mom," she'd joke, "Wanna come dancing with me at the gay bar? Or how about the Noir Leather sex show at Club X? Come on, Mom, just this once? It's Christmas after all!"

"That's enough of that kind of talk," her father would input, sticking his head in the kitchen doorway, pointing the TV remote at Leigh herself, as if it could somehow wield the same power on her as the fuse box once had.

This year, Leigh knows she will go with her mother. But she hasn't budged on her stance for nearly eight years, and to go without even a fake fight for the fun of it doesn't seem right. Seems...too sad, resigned.

"You're going," her father says, charging into the room, the word "church" still having the power to summon him, even from the big screen. He sounds as if he's going to tear a second mouth into her throat if she even tries to open hers to banter or barter. As if he doesn't have enough faith that Leigh would know this year is different.

She picks up a thin deck of cards that happens to be sitting on the counter next to the phone and her mother's stamps and pencils. Casually, she starts shuffling. "Sure, Dad, I was planning to go..." He nods and gives one of those little Dad-grunts halfway between Yeah, Huh, and Un-uh. "...if Mom will get a tattoo with me," Leigh says, hands busy flipping through the cards, realizing it must be a euchre deck, even though her parents haven't had anyone over in some time. Leigh keeps just a sliver of eye trained on her mother to catch her smirk. As if she's been in on the joke even before Leigh.

"Well," Deborah says slowly, a puff of exasperated breath too heavy to be sincere. But Hank turns around toward Leigh, ready to fight her mother's fight. "I suppose this might be my last chance," Deborah smiles, wiping her hands slowly on a lemon tea towel. "I don't know that Saint Peter will mind so much as long as it's not skulls or daggers."

"Deborah, you're not serious," Hank reels. "You can't do any such thing. What would the doctor say? You can't just go around sticking dirty needles in your arm."

"Oh why not, at this point?" Leigh interjects, dropping a bower on the linoleum by accident, and going a little overboard in her flippant attempts to make their pain a kind of normality. But her mother doesn't seem to mind.

"The rose, is, after all," says Deborah, "a symbol of devotion. And I'm sure they're still a popular style even after all these years."

"Stop trying to take your mother to hell with you," her father says, and Leigh can't tell if he's joking or serious.

For three days Leigh flips aimlessly through art books, her mother's *Home and Garden* collection and collector's catalogues, along with a couple skin-art magazines Leigh was able to get from the corner store. She knows her mother was probably kidding right along with her. But she wants to find some kind of merging of their styles that would make a good tattoo. Something she can scan into the computer and rework while she's home. Something she can have blown up in colour and framed for her mom's bedroom wall. To make her smile when she can't get out of bed anymore.

And maybe, at some point, Leigh will put it on her own body.

The days before Christmas are hard. Leigh's older brother Ian flies home from Halifax and Deborah seems to feel the need to be up and about, even though she knows she can only handle an hour or so at a time. Deborah keeps trying to do things she can't really do anymore. Ian seems to want everything to be perfect for their Mom this year, but hasn't got the patience to help out.

"What about popcorn strings, like we used to make?" he says when Leigh is in the garage getting her parents' pre-decorated, tabletop-sized fake tree.

"What about cranberries?" he whispers in Leigh's ear as Leigh is removing the plastic-wrapped turkey heart from the butt of the bird she isn't planning to actually eat.

"What about fucking cranberries?" Leigh asks. It's her first turkey.

"Leigh..." her mother calls from her stretch on the sofa. "Do you need help in there?"

"No, Mom, I'm fine."

The sandalwood incense at the church makes Leigh's stomach lurch. Like too many years without confession, she lacks the proper preparation. She makes up lies on the spot, and not very good ones, as her mother introduces her to people Leigh probably should know, but can't remember. Most of them are much older than her mother. She can't say she works in a bar, and doesn't think they'll understand if she talks about web design. When she does tell the truth, it sounds like rehearsal to her, her voice tinny, as if she is a little girl with a tin can and a piece of wire, having an imaginary telephone conversation.

Yes, I'm the baby of the family. No, I'm not married. Yes, I live alone. Yes, across the border. No, I'm not scared at night. Yes, I'm very happy.

Leigh's mother sings in the same hollow voice Leigh uses for her small talk. Deborah's voice is alto-soprano; the notes are always just a notch out of range, and the words seem unable to quite make it past her lips. If it wasn't for her hand resting lightly on Leigh's hand, Leigh would fear she was hearing her mother from someplace much farther away. Even as it is, the pale fingers seem inconsequential as empty rubber gloves, boneless and bloodless. As if only the skin remains, creased with sixty years of washing and drying before meals. Her mother smoothes the fine hair on Leigh's wrist, rubbing at it suddenly like one might scrub at a spot on the counter. Leigh is surprised by the movement, surprised to find this floating object still attached and, on occasion, capable of all it used to be. She nods and smiles at her mother, her father looking over. She tries not to think about the next time she and her father will be in the church together.

Ian seems much better at all of this. My brother, Leigh thinks, Patron Saint of Proper Bullshit. She goes on retreat to a bathroom stall in the basement, where she admits to herself that she is probably jealous of his 100% wool, navy blue demeanour.

The tattoo is really just a photocopy of an old pencil sketch in a seed catalogue. A violet with the latin name, but to Leigh's unfeminine eye it looks like a miniature pansy, and she likes that private dualism. Both winter flowers. The violet for her mother because of that song where they represent the blood of Christ. The pansy for herself, for more obvious though unsung reasons. She presses the design between the glass and cardboard of a Clip

Art frame from the dollar store in the Dougall Street strip mall. The lines of the drawing are dark and crisp, perfect for applying to skin, but delicate and flowing as an Art Nouveau piece, an ad from before her mother was born, the kind of stuff Leigh has always thought of as nostalgia-before-it-ages. Postcardy.

Ian says a suitable but unsentimental grace. Leigh eats two servings of turkey because her dad gives her that *look*. It's dry, and Leigh wishes there were cranberries. Everyone pours an excess from Leigh's new gravy boat. Deborah says everything is a blessing, just wonderful. She starts to cry thin streams from the corners of her eyes, and Hank stands up and goes to her and kisses her full on the mouth in a way that Leigh has never seen from them. Her father's lips are the colour of fourth-cup coffee from the same pot, and her mother pecks him five or six times, and then turns her face into his shoulder for one short sob. Her pink fingers curl like shrimps on a ring around his dark flannel collar.

Leigh feels sick to her stomach. Like she's on the wrong side of the table on a TV movie set, blocking the true audience's view. My parents deserve this time, she thinks, wishing to see love for what it is. Instead, she looks at her lap.

Sunday night—her first night back at home in her own place—Leigh logs on to the Internet and goes to ebay, looking for interesting items to spend her Christmas money on. She surfs around: Vintage Clothes and Antique Jewellery. She gets frustrated and moves on to Cameras, and then somehow comes across an old toy whose description has called it up under Cameras: Viewmaster with the original storybook cards.

Leigh peers at the image on her computer screen. The binocular-like red-orange plastic. The familiar white paper wheels. Each small brown window a frame waiting for illumination. How could hours of her childhood be spent so easily, flipping the advance and watching the scene change? Nice. Hokey, but nice. It comes with the original 1970s packaging. The font is irresistible. She puts in a bid.

She moves on to Records: 12" vinyl, 45s, and portable record players from the 1940s and 50s. At around 3 a.m. it occurs to Leigh that she is really just wasting time, and that her collections aren't that far off from her mother's tea tins and thimbles, or her dad's classic model cars and Coca-Cola paraphernalia. Collections are collections, after all. Junk that you actively accumulate. Its only real value, its reminiscence.

But this kind of thinking makes Leigh feel old. As though she is actually a living part of history. She has been feeling this way for a while. One might expect this sudden time consciousness would have descended on Leigh when Deborah was diagnosed with acute ALS. The letters assigned to her weakness. The description of how her body would debilitate gradually, shut down, become limited in its motion. Yet, Leigh wasn't snagged by the realization just then. The diagnosis was more like driving through an intersection and the light turning yellow.

Leigh attributes this creeping understanding of the pull of history to what she calls America the Dying. The differences between herself and her parents are defined only by the tangible. By large objects hurtling through the atmosphere. The amount of space between point A and point B. On a map, Leigh can not comprehend what her father can.

The space between life and death is similar, requiring a legend to interpret the distance. Her parents, somehow, grasped this concept right away. Chewed on it like a piece of red meat.

America the Dying. Leigh grew up on classics, cowboy westerns on TV, and Reader's Digest Songbook, Woody Guthrie, Hank Williams and hamburgers, because those were her parents' most immediate loves. Like many immigrants, especially those who arrived young enough to be hungry for change, they were obsessed with American culture, the earlier the better. A true love-hate relationship—loved to consume it, hated to be part of it. That borderline mentality.

"Deserter," Ian had hissed half-seriously when Leigh told them she was going to take advantage of her citizenship and move back to the US. Their parents were born just before World War II and emigrated to Canada after a ten-year stopover in the US where she and Ian were born. He thought it was the most ironic thing he'd ever said, since they had left Chicago before the end of the Viet Nam war.

Hank and Deborah drove the largest cars possible made by Chrysler or Ford, went on camping trips with little side treks to anyplace in the middle of nowhere that bore the sign: Historical Site. Little brown plaques on fence posts along the highway. Long grass and nothing to see. Nothing but the yellow lettering on the markers. Places like Thamesville and Dresden, Ontario. Uncle Tom's Cabin and Jack Miner's Bird Sanctuary. Old Fort Henry. Tecumseh's Corn Festival, Leamington's Tomato Festival, Harrow County's Peach Festival. Once, Niagara Falls and Marineland. Once to the top of Lake Michigan. A cheese factory tour of Wisconsin, the Minneapolis zoo in Minnesota, and Norman Rockwell-esque North Dakota where the fields really were brown and gold patches on a quilt.

Scenic Point the sign said simply, cropping up unexpected at the edge of the road. They pulled off, stepped over the parking curb and the world fell away. Leigh clung to the rail over the Painted Valley Canyon. Tried not to imagine the feeling of plummeting.

The sky like steam above the coffee-coloured cup of the canyon. Centuries emblazoned on rock. The breath of time held there as if between cracked cupped hands.

On Monday Leigh gets up early. She's anxious to resume work on a site she's let sit over the holidays. It's a bigger company and carries a bigger payment than she's used to. If she were smart, she knows she'd move back to Windsor while keeping all her American clients, take advantage of the dismal state of the Canadian dollar. The smallness of the city. Its humble face pressed into the dark lap of America. Pay the low Windsor lunch-bucket rent and bank her inflated US income at Scotia Bank, Royal or CIBC. It hasn't been that long since she started freelancing and money's still tight, but when a job like this comes through it still baffles Leigh that anyone would pay her so much to sit in her pyjamas and move text into boxes on a screen. A few codes, and *voilà*: a product. It doesn't seem like a real product somehow, the way it would if it were a poster or brochure or book. Something shiny or shrink-wrapped.

Sure, it takes hours, and it's fussy. But it's just an image—a few collected images. Since it isn't anything tangible, she guesses she's still in the service industry after all. They pay her more for the energy she expends than for its actual outcome. How do you put a price on energy? Leigh wonders as she clicks open the Finder and searches for the name of a picture file she seems to have misplaced. Both of her parents work directly in energy. Her dad as a foreman at the hydro plant; her mom, until last year, in the office of Union Gas. The cost of keeping things running. When she finishes building this site, she'll be able to live on it for a few months. She'll be able to live on the grey-white glow of this non-product, this thing that doesn't exist.

By that night, the site is roughly complete, but Leigh's eyes are so strained she can't surf the net, read or watch TV. She didn't break all day to eat, but she doesn't feel like cooking either. She eyes the clean coral gravy boat sitting empty on the centre of the tabletop. She decides to make a centrepiece out of it, by filling it with water and setting a small white floater candle inside. She lights the candle, and fills the kettle. She makes herself some coffee and toast and takes a photo album out of her desk drawer. Sitting at the table, she starts at the back, where all her current things are.

Leigh flips quickly backwards. None of the pictures are of friends, or if they are, they're of friends who wound up becoming partners in some form or another. Maybe that's why now it doesn't seem like there is anyone she can really call. Leigh wonders why with all this love, pressed back to back, there still seems to be so little.

She can still feel the weight of bones and muscles, the fine hairs of lovers woven into her thighs. Can still feel their shapes in sleep, stencilled against her hips, their voices etched into her ears, piercing her. Yet the reality has faded. They are collected here so easily. Though she carries them around on her, they are superfluous. In their absence, beautiful abstractions. Ghosts.

Even Gage seems unreal. Though they spent years beside each other. This mating bond, supposedly the strongest between any two creatures. She can remember the white lines their bodies made side by side on the blue fabric of the bedsheets. The things they said. Yet her lovers do not know this Leigh.

This Leigh that is alone. In a city on the other side. This person whose mother is losing free will—cannot move arms or legs. This person whose mother is leaving, fading. More and more, bit by bit, every minute.

The person Leigh is now does not include Gage as a lover, a partner. It includes Gage only as Gage. She can pinpoint the flaws in people without attaching them to herself, now.

Adam: matching dish set, probably designer, $500?, Internet-ordered Fluevog shoes, $250, an imported personality into a factory town, custom-made for European pornography and dominant women. Samantha: home-grown herbs from seed packs, large terracotta pots, bright yellow kitchen paint $30/gallon, inability to separate true love from tea leaves and tarot cards. Dale: environmental activist turned apathetic, beeswax for dread-locks, $4, garage sale folding bicycle, $10, nickel bag of pot, $50.

Leigh stops on her own picture.

Leigh: bi-sexual, bi-patriot, Bi-way bargain-hunter with metropolitan tastes. Leigh: still zipped into 1992 music scene. Leigh: two existing tattoos, old Levis and khakis, loose front teeth from hitting guard rail before plung-ing into water. Leigh: mother issues, father issues, brother issues, lover issues, and an extemely tapered fear of commitment and love. Leigh: wash separately.

Beyond this page, there are only pictures of her, Ian, Hank and Deborah. Coming up with captions for her lovers eases some of the confu-sion inside her, a restlessness. Like folding up all things done and not done. But her own caption is hard enough. She closes the book before she gets to the front pages that she knows are full of old Christmases and birthdays. Seventies snapshots. Their colours harsh, dated, outgrown. Other versions of herself, her parents.

On Wednesday night, Leigh calls up Gage. Calling up an ex isn't something she does all that often, but it's unavoidable. She should have called when she was at her parents' for Christmas. If she waits any longer, she'll seem like she's avoiding something. And anyway, she has to do something besides work and worry.

She gets the answering machine. "You've reached Darcy Gage, I'm obviously not here, so you know what to do when Tinkerbell plays the chimes." Leigh can't stomach Gage's humour, that kind of outside-in-ness. *Darcy*, what a stupid name. Never mind that her own name is the ultimate e-sound, Leigh hates all names that have ie- or y-endings. *Darcy*. Plus it's one of those gender-neutral names from the '70s and '80s, the kind that sound stupid on either men or women: Jamie, Charlie, Terry/Terri, Kerry/Cary, Kelly or Corey or Stacy. Fucking *Darcy*. When they were together, it was just *Gage*, as far as Leigh was concerned. Sturdy, clean, simple.

Hearing the voice, she's half-relieved to get the machine. Maybe this wasn't such a great idea. Never mind that Darcy was the one to leave Leigh for another girl in the end, there is still always that ring of hope when they speak. As if Leigh was the one to end things and Darcy has been sitting by the phone waiting for Leigh to call and ask forgiveness. Leigh cringes at the length of the beep.

"Gage, it's Leigh. Call me back if you survived the holidays. I thought you might want to get together before New Year's. You could come over and watch old Mystery Science Theatre reruns or we could drive to Royal Oak for a real film if you want. Whatever. You know my number."

Whatever. What is she thinking? "Whatever" sounds so desperate.

Darcy calls back within the hour.

"Hi Leigh, it's good to hear from you..."

"Hey Gage."

"You know I always hated it when you called me that."

"I know."

Gage's voice sounds raised a notch, the cadence slightly stiff, impersonal, as if trying to pretend Leigh weren't an old lover, but just an old friend or workmate. She can tell that Gage's Woman must be there. Leigh thinks of her that way—The Woman—even though Leigh has once or twice in her life been the other woman herself. Maybe she thinks of her this way because her own extra-curricular lovers were never secret, weapons. They always had names.

Gage is noncommittal, but very pleasant. "I just don't know what my schedule will be this weekend, but I'll certainly call you again before then," Gage says. Leigh knows that this means it's certain she'll get a call tomorrow and they'll establish plans for Friday night when The Woman is working.

"And how is your mother?" Gage says in that phoney, show-and-tell voice. Maybe so The Woman will know that this is what still binds them, concern for Leigh's well-being. Gage and The Woman are talking about buying a house together and doing the baby thing. She wonders how The Woman thinks of her. Whether she is Gage's Unstable Ex. Maybe that fits just fine, Leigh thinks.

By Thursday night, Leigh's ready for her shift at the bar. Anything to get her out of the apartment and her own head. She's been up 'til six nearly every night doing not a whole lot, really, when she thinks about it. She gets up at noon, only has time for a shot of espresso from the place on the corner. At around eight at night, there is a lull, and she desperately wants a cigarette, but she won't. She won't, she won't, she won't, she won't. She grabs a bag of chips at the bar, even though she knows she really should take her break to go down the street for a sandwich. The idea of going out into the cold. It just doesn't seem worth it. It's a busy night and she and her co-workers bite back some lemon slices with tequila shots to keep things hopping.

When she falls into bed that night, she can feel the corners of the floor and ceiling, pulling up and down, gathering together to suspend her in a kind of hammock. She feels herself swinging, just there. Her body stretched on strings of sound. Echoes from the bar system twanging in her ears. A hard canvas sleep.

She dreams of drowning. Except that it isn't her, but one of her co-workers. They've gone skating on the river. One moment they are holding hands, all of them in a long line, like crack the whip. She has a vague sense that Gage is there too, but doesn't know why. The next minute she looks over and one of her co-workers has fallen through. All she can see are the black leather gloves, raised above the pooled hole. Gloves like her father's. Even as she is moving towards the hole, she watches as the gloves disappear, and then bob back up. She is on her belly, stretched across the cold. The sensation of water seeping into her jeans. She catches his hands and pulls to no avail.

Even in the dream, some kind of lucidity seeps through. She finds herself thinking, *after all the nights on the weight machine at the gym...I should be able to pull him up, at least partway*. But his head won't clear the water. Only his hands. She can hear the ice cracking further. Her own bare hands plunge into the water, as the gloves go under again. Then, she feels someone stretching down behind her, taking hold of her ankles, firmly.

She wakes to the telephone, groping for it frantically.

"Dad?" she says, still lying half in the bed. "Hello?"

"It's Darcy. I'm sorry, did I wake you? I forgot you still had that night shift."

"Gage. I was having this dream. I think you might have been in it. It was about my dad. At least, I think it was my dad. I had to save him, but I wasn't strong enough. What time is it?"

"Just after eleven. Sorry, look, I thought you might want to get together tonight."

"Yeah, yeah, okay." Her head and throat are slowly clearing. "I have to go to the gym, but I'll call you around eight."

"Okay, I have to run a few errands, so call my cell."

"Oh yeah, your cell. I forgot you got one of those."

"You have the number?"

She does. Somewhere.

It has been too long since she's worked out. She knows this before she takes her clothes off and sees her body in the full-length mirror of the change room. The holidays have not been kind. Leigh knows she is doing okay, comparatively, to others her age. But she doesn't feel like herself. She can see that the turkey has added an extra inch or two to her hips. Her breasts look lumpy as potatoes. She can feel the apple she ate when she got up this morning like a hard knot below her rib cage. She realizes that the 28", 28" she ordered from the catalogue isn't going to fit her when it arrives. 30 inches?

It's funny how much two inches can do. When Leigh smashed her face on the guard rail before plunging into the river, she hit the septum of her nose and jarred the teeth behind it. Two inches higher and she would have been knocked unconscious immediately.

Her mother will have to send the skirt back and reorder. Leigh feels embarrassed. This is one more thing her mother will have to do. Just because Leigh was remembering what she used to be.

There's no one in the change room, and she puts on her workout clothes slowly, watching herself in the mirror. Her dream is still bothering her. She has this notion that it's really about herself and the time she jumped in the river. That she is trying to pull herself out, not someone else. Or maybe she's more worried about her father than her mother, what will happen to him. *Who helped me?* she wonders. *At the end of the dream, who grabbed my ankles?*

She does her stretches in the change room because she doesn't like the way her body folds and creases and she doesn't want anyone to see it in those awkward shapes that seem more exposing or humiliating than any sexual position. Her legs spread, her ass in the air, her hands wrapped around her running shoes.

It's just after seven. The gym is nearly empty. It's one of the reasons Leigh chose this gym. It's not one of the ones where people tend to congregate and cruise. Because of its location, it mostly serves a daytime crowd, people between 3 p.m. and 6 p.m. That "just after work" crowd. Often older men and women. But Leigh isn't surprised to see Barbie here. Barbie isn't the girl's real name, of course, and she's not even blonde. It's just Leigh's personal label for her. Usually Barbie is here with her boyfriend Ken, and they spot each other on the weights. They are both of an indeterminate age. Too defined to be old, and too expressionless to be young. Both wear designer gym clothes and don't sweat.

Leigh decides to start in reverse order. She's been away from the gym for a whole week, and she doesn't want to jump right in with the treadmill. She wants get her heart rate going a bit first. Since she seems to have her choice of things, she starts with leg curls. She sets the weights to the easiest level, and lays on her stomach on the bench, bringing her feet nearly flush to her bum. She watches the gigantic silver needle plunge in and out of the stack of black brick weights. Feels the tension stretch from her hamstrings and up into her lower back as her knees bend and then drop straight out behind her, lowering weight down on weight with a clink, clink, clink.

She does two reps of twenty before switching to a sitting position. Much easier. Like pumping one's legs on a swing. She does one rep of ten, then increases the weight and does one rep of twenty. Leigh's never had a workout partner, so she can't be certain she does anything the right way. Whether she should be lifting less or more, quicker, slower, or how many times, she doesn't know. When she joined up, she read the machine manuals, but it was more important to her that she just be doing something. She didn't really care what or what the results were. She felt like her life had settled into a dull pattern of click-click—clunk-clunk, between the computer mouse and the bottles plopped down on the bar. As if her hands were the only part of her moving.

She switches to arm curls and then bench press. She can feel the heat of the gym. She knows she's had a week off, but she's sure it's not just her. They've obviously got the thermostat up a notch higher than usual. She hasn't even done her running and she feels a bit dehydrated. When she gets up from the bench press, she notices the sweat marks on the black leatherette, but doesn't bother wiping them off. Instead, she retrieves her water bottle, and takes a short drink, hoping it isn't going to give her cramps.

She does a few leg lunches, and then she feels ready for the electric treadmill. She usually runs about a mile, then takes the speed down to a slow walk for about a minute and a half, or else she pauses the machine and has a drink from her bottle. Then on her second mile, she feels a new energy, especially if she raises the speed to 6.0 miles per hour. The first mile is always the most difficult. It's all about rhythm. Often in her head, she is spelling out the names of people she knows. Or counting. Things that don't take much concentration and are steadier than song lyrics. The radio is always on, but it's usually some kind of dance music, not her station. Whatever nonsense comes into her head is usually better for keeping a pace.

Tonight she feels like she's really pushing it. She takes a two-minute break, and she takes it early, at three-quarters of a mile. Only seventy-one calories. She has no idea what the equivalent is in kilometres. Metric and imperial have always been mixed up for her. In winter she uses Celsius; in summer, Fahrenheit. For designing, inches; for driving, kilometres. Growing up on the border during the changeover, you would think she would understand both systems. Instead, she understands neither.

This isn't the machine she usually runs on. Hers has an Out of Order sign hanging on it. Even though they are identical, she finds this one somewhat dizzying. The position of it, she thinks. All of the equipment faces the window, and though she is used to running after dark, headlong into her own reflection, she can see in the window the murky reflection of the rest of the room surrounding her, in a way that her usual position doesn't give. Behind her are the weight machines, and behind them, a mirror, which in turn reflects a miniature version of her back, the back of her head, the bottoms of her shoes. Two opposite views of herself, and her body moving frantically, perfectly in sync, between them. The machine is turned up to 6.0 mph. Leigh just wants to get to a 1.5 distance tonight. That will be enough. But she wants to get there as quickly as possible. She doesn't think she can hold on for another ten minutes like the first.

She can feel the machine frame, shaking slightly with her impact. She feels as if she's going too fast. As if the pumping motion of her body isn't even making contact. As if she is hovering over the grey rubber ribbon spinning away beneath her feet. This running in one place. The feeling, she realizes, is not unlike treading water. She looks down, concentrating on the digital meter, the time clicking off, making the distance. Making sure her feet are centre on the belt sliding her away from herself. Then she feels it, her right shoe hits the steel frame, not the belt. The motion is of floating as she takes off, flying. Backwards. Off the machine.

When she wakes, the first voice she hears is her mother's. Not the words, just the voice. She thinks they must have both crossed over. She feels panic, like a clogging at the back of her throat. She shuts out the whiteness and she slides back under the blue-green sheet of sleep.

"I made a list of everything you might need while you're here in the hospital," Deborah says. And when Leigh hears this, she can feel her lungs expanding with air again.

Then Leigh hears her father's voice. "You were pushing yourself too hard. You passed out, Leigh. You need to learn to eat and sleep like a normal person." The words are from the back of his throat, a kind of choke-hold warning. But Leigh can feel his massive hand, gentle, stroking her hair. Like he did when she was little.

Then as she tries to move, Ian's. "They gave you an IV in that arm. You were dehydrated."

Then Gage's, hearty as a handshake, but the voice grips tight and cold-white with its attempt to be casual, as if they were just making acquaintance for the first time. "Hi Leigh." Because they were supposed to meet after, she remembers.

That whole bit about your life flashing before your eyes is bullshit, Leigh decides right then. It happens too fast. One day, these months with her mother will be mere minutes. If only Fate's name came up on the Caller ID. But really, Fate's not calling you, she realizes, her head still throbbing, her eyes half-open. Whether you've misdialled or not, you're calling Fate and it knows your number. Your number appears on the screen and Fate simply answers.

Coming to is like coming back into the world. Relief is like a hard punch to the head. Leigh's ears are ringing. She reaches out and finds a hand, detached, as far as Leigh can tell for the moment, from its body. She doesn't know whose it is. Only that it is warm and not tagged with a cord, as hers seems to be. She is vaguely aware of the plastic scratch of the admittance armband, and the limited span afforded to her by the IV needle. She grabs onto the hand, and it squeezes back. Though she can see the room now, it seems to her, just for this moment that it's very important that she not let go yet.

"I know, Leigh," her mother says very softly, though Leigh hasn't asked her anything. It's her mother's half-useless hand, connecting them. And when the time comes, they will switch places and Leigh will sit where she sits. On the other side of the bed. Everything else will be set aside. She will be ready. Just by being there. "I know," her mother says again, just a touch louder, though they are still in the same room.

THE YEARS OF THE
STRAWBERRY CIRCUS

THE FIRST TIME I met Josh, he was talking about self-love—masturbation really. And isn't it just a form of narcissism? Don't most women fantasize by looking in the mirror? The way Josh said it, it wasn't much of a question.

Brenda went on to talk about using her pillow and her stuffed bear, Miriam closed her eyes as if she was going to throw up, and this hippie guy muttered that the problem with masturbation was that you could never kiss your own mouth. But conversations like that happened all the time, in bars or on street corners and after a while the colours of passing people and the strains of their voices blurred together. Josh was just background.

But he kept popping up. The first time after that, I think, was on the bus and it was raining. The smells of people sitting so close had gotten mixed up the way they do: sweat and newsprint, coffee steam from paper cups, hairspray, overdone aftershave, a whiff of rubber boots, urine, base-ment. Wet, restless, excited. I didn't notice he was there until he pulled the cord and stood up. He zipped up his jacket and jumped out into the pissy rain without my having to say hi. The bus lurched past him, and the day moved on, into other days.

I was still living with Miriam then. Here in Windsor, of course. On South Street, just a block behind the Chippewa Tavern. Remember a few years back, that couple on trial for killing their baby? They used to live just a block up, on Peter. So you get the idea. Our whole neighbourhood was depressing. Even three-year-olds would teeter out onto their porches to tell us to fuck off. We rode the bus a lot, me and Miriam. Neither one of us could afford a car. Miriam changed jobs from week to week and I mostly borrowed from my parents. We pretended to be high school girls so we could get a student bus rate, and on weekends, or particularly grungy afternoons we went drinking downtown. On one or two Saturday nights at places with bands and cover charges, Miriam promised she'd go down on the door guy, and we ducked in for free, and out again before last call, before he could try to collect. But at our regular bars, they got to know our faces, and we didn't have to bring our ID. We always wore jeans and when skinny bar girls in dresses walked by, Miriam would turn to me and say, Let them eat cake. Then we would try to get everyone in the bar jigging, if it happened to be a pseudo-Irish band, and if it wasn't, we would sit in the corner and talk about love because we didn't have any. Or the politics of sisterhood, if it happened to be a particularly bad night. Or sometimes someone we knew would offer to share some pot with us in the alley, and then my hair would become a living thing on my head, little lights at the tips of strands, which tickled when I touched them. That was where we were coming from—where I was coming from.

And in the day I ran into him on the street. All the time I started seeing him. He worked at a downtown restaurant, the kind appealing to Casino tourists and American businessmen, its patio extending into the sidewalk. As I was carousing with Miriam, or running meagre errands alone, he would be shouldering trays the size of tables, food to feed armies of businessmen. He would glide out over the railing with forty pounds balanced on a shoulder no wider than mine, and never miss a beat, sweep the whole load down in one motion, dishes delicately placed by some other sudden hand. And somehow, he always noticed me passing by and found the breath midsweep for an unbroken hello.

You have to say hello back in a situation like that. You're too awed to ignore it. I had to, anyway. Miriam didn't remember ever meeting him, even after I reminded her. Oh, she said, as though it had happened to someone else. I remembered because I had seen him so often since, but also because the pieces didn't match up.

The day that Miriam left for Toronto, we took a cab downtown to the train station. She had a suitcase and an old hockey bag of her brother's. She wasn't taking any furniture. It was all from yard sales and wasn't worth the trouble. We weren't late and we probably could have managed the stuff on the bus, but we took the cab anyway. It felt like we should do something different, something to remind ourselves before it happened.

We stood in line and bought her ticket together. I owed her money for the groceries that were still sitting in the fridge. We had twenty minutes until her train, and we spent it reading the personals to each other, laughing at how people define themselves.

Then she stood up and hoisted her bags all around her so I couldn't hug her. Unless she initiated it, Miriam was opposed to contact. She had endured it once or twice from me, always stiffening and retreating quickly. Well, I hate goodbyes, she said, shifting her weight from foot to foot.

See you later, I said.

Yeah, see you.

She turned to walk away to put her things on the train, and I didn't hug her. I let her go, watching the back of her head, I thought about how fast her hair had grown and how the next time I saw her she would have it long enough to pull back.

She called a couple days later. She had left some things behind, things she needed right away, she said. They were mostly odds and ends: thick-framed sunglasses, a cup, a book of scraggly cat drawings, a few magazines and homemade tapes, the pair of scissors with the green handles, and she'd decided she wanted the kitchen clock after all. The clock had a picture of Strawberry Shortcake on its face, and as I pulled it down I noticed the orange brush strokes all around the outside. Miriam had left it up and painted around it. I found the other things on her shelves or in her chest of drawers. Our stuff had gotten mixed up after three years together. I had been missing the cassettes for some time. The scissors were mine too. I put them in the box with the other things and mailed them to her.

A couple months later, I quit scamming student loans for the college classes I never attended. I took a full-time job waitressing. I thought of him sometimes at the end of shifts I'd been busiest. It bothered me that I couldn't remember his name, especially after he'd said hello so many times. But more than that, I thought about what kind of person it takes to say hello to an almost stranger in the middle of rush hour with forty pounds of dishes hovering overhead. I hadn't seen him in a long time, he must have quit the job at the restaurant downtown.

Miriam called sometimes. She had become quite the bar bunny though, and kept a lot of boys coming and going at her whim, so I didn't call her much—it always seemed to be an inappropriate moment. I wondered how she got away with the things she got away with. She found ways to meet boys no matter where she was—at night at concerts, and in the day at the post office, the subway station, the falafel hut. It wasn't her fault, she said, I wasn't around to keep her in line. Toronto was huge without me, and when was I coming anyway?

I didn't have an answer for that one, and she knew better than to ask twice. There was nothing really holding me to this town. Nothing but the rent and the lease, my unexplainable attachment to the chimney sweep flavour of Windsor's characters. But none of that has any hold really. Money, promises, love. There are ways to forget about those things. They were excuses and Miriam knew it.

This town is swallowing us whole, she said to me the night she decided to leave. She didn't say it again.

I finally went to see her in Toronto. She had gotten herself into some drama program there. I could have visited her before. I had lots of friends who wouldn't have minded a weekend road trip, or wanted someone to split the gas money. But whenever I wasn't working, Miriam had exams or auditions, and when she finished those, I was working again. That was an excuse too, and I knew it even at the time. Even after I found a replacement roommate, in my head it was still Miriam's Room. As much as she wanted me to join her in Toronto, I wanted her to come back here.

Nights when I was way too drunk I called her from the bar and left long messages on her answering machine. I can't remember what I said, probably nothing, but I remember holding myself in bed afterwards, unable to move my legs, and thinking, if I have to throw up I won't even be able to get out of bed. Then I would start to shake, believing I must have alcohol poisoning and if only Miriam were still living here, she would know what to do. I'm going to die, I thought. I'm going to die, I'm going to die.

Miriam left messages too, but even stoned or depressed she seemed whimsical. Oh, she said into the machine, It's raining today and I'm all out of oranges and that really made me sad so I thought I would call and now you aren't home either. I bought a whole bunch of Clementines last week and they were so perfect and today I didn't have any money for lunch, so I was looking forward to getting home and eating oranges and drinking this fabulous licorice root tea I got. But I forgot I ate the last ones a couple nights ago, in bed with this stupid intellectual boy I brought home. He had a goatee, and I know you're cringing and saying, a goatee? But he had a huge bag of weed and he wanted to talk about Foucault, and at the time it seemed so exciting. Now it just seems smarmy and pathetic. Foucault, Derrida. Oh so much for my week. I'm just babbling. You have to call me back and tell me something real.

After weeks of one-sided conversations I was surprised when she actually picked up.

Miriam? I asked her.

Yeah, who else would it be?

Fuck, I told her, That's it.

And I gave in and bought the ticket the next day.

She had class when my bus got in so I spent the afternoon knocking around the shops on Queen. But honestly, the dollar stores all down Yonge were more my style. We had agreed to meet at a coffee shop. I found the place easily, about thirty minutes early. I read a freebie paper.

Love is love is love, my horoscope scolded me. You have been hiding your feelings from yourself. You will find consequences quietly kept in drawers among the forks.

I saw Miriam before she saw me. She was standing kitty-corner to the café among six or seven other people waiting to cross. She was wearing a green and white polka dot scarf over her hair, and the thick-framed sunglasses I had mailed back to her. A pink raincoat and red lipstick. She looked like a 1950s movie star between February's black and grey hats and coats. The window was half steamed up and I saw the colour before I saw her face. Crossing the street, her steps seemed too long for her body, her hands thrust deep in her pockets, like she'd just as soon be anywhere.

I stood up when she came in, but she saw me as soon as her hand hit the door. Fancy running into you here, she said. She leaned over and kissed me on the cheek, leaving lipstick on me as if I was her boyfriend.

Her apartment was on Carleton and Jarvis, and turned out to be one room for living and sleeping. There was also a kitchen the size of a bathroom and a bathroom the size of a cubicle. She had rag-rolled the walls the colour of caramel corn and left masking tape running along the baseboards. A nail hole in the wall was the size of my thumb, evidence of poor plaster. So the Strawberry Shortcake clock had been hung by a string from the kitchen door handle. She had scattered bay leaves by the sink to combat cockroaches. But it was something she didn't share with anyone else. The dishes were hers, the telephone was hers, the Klimt and Dali posters taped to the walls, the cupboards stocked with potatoes and peanut butter, the bathtub and blackberry bubble bath, the kitchen table in the middle of the living room—all hers.

She got self-conscious and began picking up the towels and clothes that were strewn from the bathroom to the bed.

I lived with you, I teased her.

Oh yeah, she said. She dumped the clothes into one pile in the corner. Well, what do you think, then?

It's beautiful, I told her.

We went out that night and got sloppy drunk with an armful of Miriam's friends. She excitedly introduced me to everyone: Carey, Michelle, Ella, and Slav. She joked with them like she had known them forever. I don't know what I had expected. She had this new life somewhere else and I was still in the same life she'd left me in. I took charge by filling everyone's glasses again and again.

Carey, the girl sitting next to me asked me how Miriam and I had wound up as roommates. She kept stealing my boyfriends, I told her.

Carey looked like she didn't believe me. She asked if I was masochistic. Why would I ever move in with someone who stole my boys?

I figured we must have something in common, I confided.

She didn't understand. Didn't you date anyone? she wanted to know, Didn't you get lonely?

Not really. I lived with Miriam. What other entertainment could I need? Besides, I said, I learned to masturbate really, really well.

It was springtime when I saw him again. I had quit the job at the restaurant. It was raining again, after a long afternoon of hiking around with resumés and bad shoes. My hair was wet and hairgel stringy and my feet were aching. It was just turning night. I walked towards this place with a green and white awning. I hadn't been there before but the sign above the door advertised the Corktown Criers with opening band Johnny Cum Lately. The place seemed too mom-and-pop for either band. An orange neon sign declared Bar & Grille from the window.

When I walked in the tables were still cluttered from the dinner rush. He was there. He was carrying a grey plastic bus-bin, clanking spoons into cups, clattering knives onto plates.

He recognized me but couldn't place me right away. He wiped the tabletop in front of me, balancing the bin of dishes against his hip with his other arm. There was a beer bottle and I saw that it was going to topple. With restaurant-quick hands we both swiped for it. It deflected off my fingers and he caught it in his dishrag hand.

He set the bottle in the corner of the bin. He asked me if I was Miriam's friend. He said his name was Josh.

He mentioned Miriam's hair, how he remembered her because he used to be able to see her coming from halfway down the street. All that red hair.

I nodded. Before it got trendy she couldn't find dye that colour, and she used to use Kool-Aid. She would stain her lips with it too.

He set the bin on the bar and gathered clean glass ashtrays to glide onto the tables. That's right, he said, I remember the two of you looked completely mismatched next to each other. Like opposites. She always looked like she was on some nasty trip, and you, well, you look like you haven't gone yet.

Hey, I protested, I'm not that naive.

Oh, I don't mean it that way. I don't mean it that way at all.

He didn't tell me what he did mean. And I didn't ask. He was humming two stray lines of a pop song over and over, and I decided there were worse places to be. Josh poured me another coffee, heavy on the Irish cream. He didn't charge me. I wondered if it was an apology.

It felt good to sit in on the in-between stuff. He was so casual it made me feel welcome, like I came in every day for that coffee, or like I worked there too. He moved around the room like he owned it, swinging chairs into place, clunking their wooden legs against each other. He had the place in order before I could even start the second drink.

Johnny Cum Lately got there late, a bunch of high-school boys in plaid pants. A lot of safety pins. I thought they might have something intelligent to sing, but it turned out they just wanted to be rock stars. I had seen Corktown Criers several times before with Miriam. They were from Detroit, with put-on accents. Maybe the singer had an Irish grandfather. But it didn't matter. They knew how to make some danceable noise. And more and more people were drawn in. I finished my second, then my third Irish cream, and ordered a pint. I watched the bar fill up.

A girl with Raggedy Ann braids was hopping up and down in front of the blasting speaker, flopping her head from side to side. She had a Guinness in one hand and her other arm across the shoulder of another girl, a shadow thrown from her. They were moving together, laughing under the spotlight, the Raggedy Ann girl's mouth open and red, her eyes wild. Fuck it, she was saying, laughing. Fuck it. This is it.

Josh picked up my empty pint glass. Dark or pale ale, he wanted to know.

That girl, I said in his ear, pointing and gripping his forearm. That girl.

He looked confused, followed my finger. Yeah? he asked.

She looks like my friend.

Yeah, he said. Yeah she does. Wherever you go there's always someone like her.

No, I told him. There isn't.

No, he said. He could only half-hear me, and he was distracted, trying to get the drink orders and collect the empties. He asked me if I wanted anything.

I want to go dance with her, I said, still clutching his shirt sleeve.

Okay, you go dance with her.

No. She's gone you know.

Josh nodded and twisted away from the table into the crowd looking for other drink orders. He came back a few songs later. He brought me a coffee without any liqueur. I had been discreetly cut off.

He set it down in front of me. Wherever you go, you see those people around, he said, because you take them with you. He touched my shoulder and moved away.

I didn't see either Josh or Miriam again while I lived on South Street. Of course I would have seen her at Easter, but she had strep throat and didn't want to bus home. A friend from high school, Andrew, had opened a sandwich shop in the east end, and promised me as many hours as I wanted. I was ready to call it quits with the replacement roommates I'd had since Miriam. A place in the east end would be quiet, a balcony-sized step up, especially from South Street. I found that if I quit going out at night, somehow it was enough for a decent apartment. I didn't know what to do with the bulky pink davenport or the fake wood end tables Miriam had lugged home from the Goodwill. Even though I had used them more than she had, I felt like I was cleaning up after her.

Throw them out, she said when I called and asked her. She said she was going to Ireland. What? When? I had talked to her just a couple weeks before.

Oh love, can't you just see me there? We're talking a culture that has deified wide-hipped women and beer! Imagine me jigging to the real stuff and drinking with the people. I'm going to hitchhike across the entire country and back.

But how are you getting there? I asked.

It's this boy, she said. He and his girlfriend broke up so he has an extra ticket. One way.

Well, how would you get back? I asked.

She didn't answer.

I left her couch and tables in the apartment for the landlord. I wanted someone to clean up after me for once.

When you move into a new place, it's hard to think of it as yours. You have to decide where to put the furniture, the pictures, clock, and the hook for the colander. In my new apartment there wasn't a nail hole that hadn't been puttied and painted over. There wasn't any history, and I hadn't brought much with me.

I ate at the sandwich shop every day. Even in the beginning we had some okay times there. Me and my friend Andrew and his girlfriend Lynn. Lynn and I liked to gang up on Andrew. We teased him all day and he would act dejected, knocking the mop handle noisily against the booths. But by nighttime, I would be mopping, knocking around, while the two of them were laughing in the kitchen.

How can you not like mayonnaise? I would hear Lynn ask him, and the threatening sound of the lid being unscrewed. Yummy, she would say, and I would hear him gagging. I could imagine her licking a gloppy spoonful of it to disgust him, or jamming it towards him. In some ways they always seemed like friends instead of a couple, the way Miriam and I always seemed like a couple instead of friends.

Miriam never did go to Ireland. The boy and his girlfriend got back together before the departure date. Miriam called me up at the restaurant in the middle of the day.

I'm moving to Espanola, she said.

Is that in New Mexico?

No, Ontario. It's a little town near Sudbury.

What's wrong with Toronto?

It's Toronto, she said and I could almost hear her tossing her candy-apple head.

Well, what's in Espanola?

I don't know. What keeps you where you are? She sounded fed up with me. If there's nothing to do, I'll just make something up. I think I'll be their town eccentric.

And that's what she did. I didn't ask her to come back and live with me, and she knew I wasn't going to follow her.

I got a photo from her in the mail maybe a half a year later. I don't remember her taking it. You can see the Strawberry Shortcake clock on the wall above me, and the map of the world pinned to the yellow refrigerator. I remember Miriam had drawn a big black X across the whole map and written YOU ARE HERE. In the picture, it doesn't show up, but I can see it anyway.

I'm standing at the counter, doing the dishes. She must have said my name to make me turn around so she could take the picture. My mouth is halfway open, like I was singing, or saying something to her. I look like I just woke up.

I took the picture and taped it to the fridge. It's a picture of me, but Miriam took it, so it's a picture of her too.

ACKNOWLEDGEMENTS

I've always hated books that go on and on, thanking friends and mentors for withstanding their madness while they were at work on their writing. As if writing a bunch of stuff were so tedious they could barely stand it themselves... Or as if they are looking back in wonderment of what has been accomplished. If we are writers, it seems the natural outcome. Isn't this what we're *supposed* to do? However, since everyone else is doing long acknowledgements this season, I'll send a few head nods and kisses to the following:

Brian Joseph Davis for cover and author photographs, and for pointing out to me that I might have more luck with prose than poetry. For being my very first reader—fiction and otherwise—always.

Stephen Cain for selecting my manuscript and treating it with gentle hands. For friendship, free coffees and faith. Mike O'Connor, Richard Almonte and Jan Barbieri at Insomniac Press with enormous respect. Anne McDermid & Associates, including Kelly Dignan and Nathan Whitlock.

The editors of *Queen Street Quarterly*, *THIS Magazine*, *SubTerrain*, *Blood & Aphorisms*, where some of these stories were previously published.

Ontario Arts Council for grants, and the publishers who served as recommenders.

The people who provided both insight and distraction—Viviane Kertesz; Jennifer Heyns; Sean K. Robb; Tom and Jo Schultz; Sarah Van Sinclair for banana bread; and Craig Stephen who first took me to the Ulster Coin Wash and showed me the best place in the market to buy espresso beans.

The people who provided a beginning place—my Windsor gang; machyderm; Lenore Langs; Wanda Campbell; John Ditsky; Peter Stevens; and Marty Gervais.

Thank you especially to my harshest critics and best of friends—Sean Sexsmith, Dan Robinet, Dave Stewart, and James Cowper. Also, with love, Chris Mangin. Thank you all for bearing witness to my follies.